EMER

CLOVER SPRINGS MAIL ORDER BRIDES 4

RACHEL WESSON

LONDONGATE PUBLISHING

❀ Created with Vellum

CHAPTER 1

KANSAS, 1881

"How about you give us a kiss, Sugar? It'd sure make this slop taste better."

Tempted as she was to throw the pot of beans over him, Emer wasn't that brave. Her mother had taken the strap to her the last time she had given Bill lip.

Her whole body stiffened as she imagined what he might do to her. His eyes gleamed as he spat tobacco juice out the corner of his mouth. She was scared of him. She tried to hide her fear but they both knew he knew. She saw it in his eyes.

She had seen just how cruel he was when one of his own gang had gotten shot on a raid. Instead of going for a doctor or even letting her help the injured man, he'd let his friend die in agony. She could still hear the man screaming, begging to be put out of his misery. Bill had laughed, an evil sound that pierced the very center of her heart. How she wished she didn't have to see him every day.

She bit her tongue and put a smile on her face. "Would you like some, Fred?" She ducked as Fred's boot came flying at her. They were drunk again and drink made them nasty. In her haste to escape, she tripped and fell, sprawling in the mud. "Looks like she wants more than a kiss Bill." Fred laughed at his own joke.

Emer scrambled to get away, the pot of beans left behind her. To the sound of their ribald laughter, she ran and kept running until she couldn't go any further. Panting heavily, she turned around to check if any of them had followed her. They hadn't. She was safe. For now.

She rested for a few minutes, wondering where her ma had got to. Patty knew how much she hated being alone with the men but she didn't care. All she cared about was where her next drink came from. Emer brushed away the sole tear running down her cheek. Crying was for babies and she was way too old to be giving in to a pity party. She would be fifteen next month.

Ripe for marrying, according to Bill. She shuddered as the image of his face filled her head. He was filthy, not just in mind but in body, too. The others didn't bathe that often but at least they went to the barber for the occasional shave and hair cut. Bill's hair was almost as long as hers. It was impossible to tell his hair color, it was so greasy. If he sat in the sun too long, she could probably fry an egg on his head. She giggled for a few seconds before her smile slid from her face. There was nothing to laugh about.

She pulled herself together and headed back to the house. If she kept away from the camp round the front, she would hopefully avoid Bill. Walking into the kitchen, she heard voices. Ma had company. She expected Emer to get lost when she was entertaining. She was about to leave when she heard her name. Curiosity overcame common sense. She tiptoed to the door to listen.

"You know I'm right, Patty. A fresh girl like Emer will make us a fortune. Those blonde curls and baby blue eyes. They're every fella's dream."

"Alfie, she's so innocent."

"That's what makes her special. Dora will train her so she knows what to do to keep the fellas happy. Just like her ma."

Emer hugged her arms across her chest. He couldn't mean Dora from the Silver Garter tavern. That lady had eyes as hard as rocks.

She strained closer trying to hear more.

"I dunno. She's my baby girl." Ma's voice sounded doubtful.

"You ain't got much choice. Bill has his eye on her

and he'll take what he wants for free. At least this way, you get something out of it."

"But selling her?"

"Don't go all high and mighty on me now, Patty. We both know it ain't the first time you dumped one of your girls."

Emer let her breath out. Ma wouldn't sell her. Would she? Any doubts she had soon disappeared.

"I left Sorcha with my ma. She's a good Catholic woman. She'll bring her up properly. I didn't sell her." Ma fell silent. Emer moved closer to the door, trying to listen better. When she heard the bedcovers rustling, she took a step back. A couple of minutes later, Ma spoke again. "How much would Dora pay?"

Emer's hand flew to her mouth as Alfie chuckled.

"Not sure what the going rate is. Would be better if we had her sister, too, especially if she looks like Emer. What age is she?"

"Seventeen, I reckon. No way my ma would let her go so you best get that idea out of your head."

"I dunno. I'm quite persuasive. I could go see your ma and convince her to let the girl reunite with her real ma. I could tell her you are broken-hearted without your little girl at your side."

Emer almost laughed. Her ma? Heartbroken. That would be the day!

"Come on, Patty, what you say?"

Emer recoiled at the sound of kissing.

"A little bit of cash could set us up nicely. You're getting on – all that liquor is taking its toll. It's time we set down roots. And get married."

"Nah, don't get hasty. We don't need a preacher, do we, girl? We do fine together."

Emer heard her ma crying. Crocodile tears. She'd seen her turn on the water works more often then she remembered. In the past, it meant she got her own way.

"Don't go wasting that crying act on me. I got better things to be doing. You think about what I said. You got debts to clear, Patty, and I've been patient. I want my money."

Emer hid in the shadows. She heard the man get up and swear when he couldn't find his boots. She didn't move until Alfie rode off. Then she went in to confront her mother.

CHAPTER 2

BOSTON 1881

Lawrence was glad he had decided to walk. The streets were blocked. Countless cabs and buggies stood waiting for the crowd to pass. He continued walking, wondering why so many people had gathered. Spotting a casual acquaintance, he walked toward him.

"What's going on, Cooper? Any idea?"

"Some demonstration over workers' rights again. Don't these people know they are lucky to have a job? If they don't want to work, we can find others that do."

Some workers and their families marched past them. Lawrence was amazed to see women and children marching with the men. They looked pitifully thin and their clothes, if you could call them that, resembled rags.

"These people have jobs. Why do they look as if they are starving?"

"I don't know, Shipley. They spend it all on liquor. Who knows? And frankly, who cares? Where are the police? I will be late for my dinner engagement at this rate."

Unlike Cooper, he was curious as to why working men would take time out of their day and lose wages to hold a demonstration. He moved closer to what seemed to be the center of the marchers, holding a handkerchief to his nose as the smell of unwashed bodies became intolerable.

In the distance, he heard whistles. He sensed panic and desperation as the crowd around him surged forward, walking closer together. He heard a man address the people around him. "Easy, now, no need to push. It's a peaceful demonstration. You have nothing to fear."

Lawrence had seen enough. He turned away from the direction the crowd was heading and moved toward the direction of home.

He hadn't made much progress when the police arrived. Without warning, they charged the crowd. Stunned by their actions, Lawrence couldn't move. He watched as panic spread through the crowd and chaos ensued. A small child tripped. He would have been trampled if his mother hadn't dragged him to his feet. A policeman hit a man near him, causing him to fall to the ground. His wife and children threw themselves at the policeman who then used his truncheon to defend himself.

A blow hit a child, causing a wide gash to open on his forehead. Lawrence reacted without thinking. He grabbed the truncheon from the policeman's hand and threw it to the ground. Another man hit the policeman, who fell to the floor. Lawrence jumped in front of the men and the policeman. He mightn't agree with the officer using his truncheon on the crowd but he wasn't about to leave him defenseless, either.

"Enough. Take your family home. Now. This is only going to get worse. Your child needs a doctor."

The worker he addressed stared at him sullenly for a couple of minutes before walking away, dragging his wife and child behind him. His friends followed them, leaving Lawrence to help the policeman back to his feet.

"You best get home, Sir, before someone arrests you."

Lawrence didn't get a chance to respond as the policeman rushed off back to the center of the action.

Dusting himself down, he walked home deep in thought. If working families were this badly off, how did those without a job survive?

"Lawrence Shipley, why can't you behave?"

Lawrence didn't answer the rhetorical question.

"How many times do I need to remind you of our position in society?"

"Mother, I couldn't stand by and watch as women and children were beaten. It was a peaceful protest. Until the police arrived."

"You cannot behave like this. Look at the state of your clothes! Is that blood?"

Lawrence looked down at his trousers. It could be blood or mud. He wasn't sure and it wasn't as if his mother cared, anyway.

"You cannot get involved in public demonstrations. The laws reflect the wishes of the people."

"Do they, Mother?"

His mother ignored him. She continued her lecture. "It reflects badly on your father."

Dorothea Shipley stared at her son. Lawrence stared back. Unlike the rest of the household, he wasn't afraid of his mother, a fact not lost on the woman standing in front of him. The door opened and his father walked into the room.

What's he doing home so early? Lawrence's mouth went dry as he tried to resist the urge to leave the room.

"Lawrence, we have tried to be patient. I convinced your mother we should turn a blind eye to your reckless behavior. You are a young man and I believed you would mature."

Lawrence stiffened at the censure in his father's gaze.

"At your age, Roger had completed five years as manager of Shipley Bank. He was engaged to be married to a wonderful girl from a fine family."

Saint Roger. He was not going to stand here and listen to his parents' glowing commentary on his elder brother. He moved, but his father's stern gaze gave him pause.

"We have decided to give you one final chance. Roger has agreed to train you in all aspects of banking. You will work under his guidance for the next two years. Only then will I consider entertaining this wish of yours to go west."

"Father, please. You know I have no wish to join the bank. I want to work with Grandpa Joe."

"Your grandfather agrees with me."

He couldn't. He wouldn't. Would he?

"I can see you are surprised. Joseph is a smart man. He believes you need to grow up. You are immature and lacking in moral fiber. You spend your days gallivanting from one place to another playing pranks."

"This wasn't a prank. Father, people got hurt. I only stepped in when I saw a man hit a child."

"The child had no place being there."

Lawrence opened his mouth but closed it again.

There was no point trying to explain to his parents the sights he had seen in Boston. They only wanted to see the nice side of the city.

"There is no purpose to your life. You have a role to fulfill. If you truly wish to take over from your grandfather, he insists you complete this two-year program first."

Lawrence slumped into the chair. He idolized his grandfather and thought the man held him in high regard. To hear his father tell him the person he loved most thought him immature and irresponsible was devastating. He struggled to breathe, never mind listen to what his father was saying.

"Your grandfather has requested you do not contact him until you have completed your training. Like me, he is disappointed at your lack of ambition."

Lawrence looked at his father, wondering if he knew how his words devastated him. The cold stare gave away nothing.

"You will start on Monday."

Lawrence didn't answer. He didn't stand when his parents left the room. He couldn't trust his legs to support him. Since he could remember, all he ever wanted was to live with his grandparents.

He adored his Grandpa Joe and loved spending time with him. Unlike his parents, his grandpa didn't play favorites but treated Roger and himself the same. In later years, Roger had preferred to stay in Boston.

Lawrence had spent every school holiday with his grandfather, only coming back to Boston when his parents insisted.

Grandpa Joe had taught him how to ride, how to shoot and how to survive in the wild. Not that he got a chance to use these skills in Boston. He wanted to be like his grandfather. He had built a successful business from nothing.

In the circles his parents moved in, a gentleman was one who dressed well, had completed his education and had a career. Grandpa Joe had no time for the politics of the Boston social scene. He didn't even visit Boston except for family events such as Roger's wedding.

He'd thought Grandpa Joe would understand. He didn't differentiate between men based on the color of their skin. He had said over and over, it was the color of a man's heart that was the true test of character. Yet, this same man was insisting his grandson become a banker. Enter a career he hated. It involved making rich men richer.

Lawrence pulled at his collar. He couldn't breathe. The thought of spending the next two years working in the bank in close proximity to the brother he despised was horrendous. He wouldn't do it. He would leave today. Run away. What would that prove? No, he had to stay. He wasn't going to prove his parents and his grandfather right.

He sat for a while, gathering his thoughts. He had a chance to make his grandfather proud. He would become the best banker his family had seen. Once the two years were complete, he would leave Boston and pursue his dream of setting up his own business. In the meantime, he would work harder than ever before.

CHAPTER 3

KANSAS 1881

"I should have left you with your sister, you unruly brat."

"Sister? What sister?"

Patty didn't want to answer and stuck her head back in her glass of booze

"Ma, I asked you a question. Do I have a sister? Where is she? What's her name?"

Emer didn't see the slap coming until it was too late. Her ears roared as her head rang from the impact.

"Don't you give me lip! I am still your ma."

"Aren't I the lucky one?" Emer spat back but this time she stayed far out of reach.

"What ya doing, listening to conversations that ain't none of your concern? I told you to feed the boys and do the washing."

Emer neatly sidestepped away from her mother's

outstretched arm. Once she was far enough not to be belted, she said, "You were talking about me and my sister. The one I didn't know I had. Or is it only one?"

"You watch your tongue, girl, or I will just call Bill. Yeah, we both know he'd love to put you over his knee."

"Ma, please. You ain't going to give me to Dora, are you?

"No, of course not, love. You're my baby girl. Come here and give me a cuddle."

Emer tried not to gag as she hugged her mother. Sweat and whiskey didn't make a good combination.

"Now, go on and get me something to eat. Why don't you sit with me?"

Emer went to get her ma a plate but her own appetite had disappeared. Ma was only ever nice when she wanted something.

"Ma, I got to go get some water and feed the animals. I'll be back later."

CHAPTER 4

Emer grabbed her shawl and left before her ma could argue. It was too dangerous to stay. Now that Ma knew she had heard her talk with Alfie, she could turn her over at any time to Dora.

She walked and walked until she found herself almost at the Newmark homestead. As she was walking, her thoughts strayed to her first meeting with the Newmarks. She had busted her arm and Ma, in a rare show of maternal devotion, had taken her to see the Newmarks.

Pa Newmark had served as an army surgeon during the war. He came home but hadn't been able to practice medicine. Said he'd seen enough blood to last a lifetime. He'd taken pity on the scrawny kid, though, and splinted her arm properly. Without his help, Emer doubted her arm would have healed so well. She had grown very fond of the man who taught her so much about healing herbs. Although he refused to practice medicine, he wasn't averse to using his knowledge to help those he loved including the animals on his farm. Emer soaked up his knowledge like a bison drank water after a drought.

Despite being aware of her ma's reputation, Pa Newmark saw her interest was genuine. He taught her how to clean wounds and tend to basic illnesses. He had died almost two years previously and Emer still missed him. He and Ma Newmark had made her early life just about bearable. She knew Ma Newmark had hopes for a match between her and Harvey but she didn't see the youngest Newmark that way. Besides, Patty would never agree. The Newmarks didn't have anything she needed.

Thinking of Harvey, she almost fell over his feet as he lay beside the fire he'd lit. He was sleeping outside as he often did.

"Harvey, I got to get away and you're going to help me."

"Why you got to get away? You done something?"

Emer played with a stone on the ground. She hadn't done anything. Yet. But if Bill kept up the way he was going, she was likely to kill him.

"No, I haven't done anything but I might. I have to get away. I hate that gang. You know I do."

Emer struggled to think clearly. What could she do

to get away? Maybe someone would be interested in her knowledge of the Bainstreet Gang and the loot they had hidden on the Half Circle Ranch. There could be a reward. She'd use the money to go to Boston and look for Ma's family.

"What's cooking inside that pretty head of yours?"

"I could go to the sheriff. I heard he's a tough nut but fair. He'd get me a pardon in return for what I know about Bill and the boys."

"You're likely to get shot first. You know Bill wouldn't let you talk to the sheriff."

"He doesn't have to know, does he? He doesn't know where I am now."

"Well, I guess he don't but is that what you want?"

"Maybe."

"But that would mean ratting out your ma and regardless of how bad she is, she's the only family you got."

Emer stared at the fire. He might not be the smartest guy in the world yet he had hit her exact problem. Her ma. She couldn't hand her over to the law. But he wasn't as smart as he thought was he. He didn't know everything.

"But she ain't, is she? I got myself a sister." She let the shock register before she continued. "Ma left her in Boston with our granny. She might be still there." Emer picked at a stick. What did her sister, Sorcha, look like?

"She might but she could be dead. Anyways, you can't just show up. What if she don't want ya?"

"She will. She's my sister."

"Patty's your ma and she don't seem to care too much about ya. Not from where I'm standing."

She didn't have time to hide her hurt.

"Oh, rats. Sorry, Emer. I didn't mean to hurt ya. I love ya. You know I do. Why can't you marry me? Then you'd be safe. I won't let no one touch ya."

"Yeah, I know. I can't marry you, Harvey. I'm only fifteen. I'm not ready to be a ma yet. I want to see something of the world."

"Where you going to go?"

"I'm going to find my sister. She'll help me. I know she will." She kissed him quickly on the cheek. "I need your help, Harvey. You'll have to ride with me – just to Leadville. I can get a job there. When I've saved enough money, I will go on to Boston. I can't travel alone. Not out here."

"Leadville is full of miners. You won't be safe there."

"I can look after myself. I can shoot straight. The last time we went to Leadville, Ma commented on the number of new businesses."

"I don't like it but I don't like Bill even more. I'll help you go, Emer. But you remember, I am here if you ever need me. Anytime you want to come home to Kansas, I'll be waiting right here. You just see."

Emer fought the urge to stay with him. Her instincts told her to find her missing sister. Start over. A new life where nobody knew she was Patty's daughter.

"I'm going tomorrow, Harvey, and I ain't never coming back. I mean it. As God is my witness." Picking up a stick, she idly poked the dying embers. She shivered, but not with the cold. This was it. She was never coming back to the Half Circle Ranch. Even if her sister didn't want to know her. Bill and the rest of his gang could go to ... Ma, too.

CHAPTER 5

LEADVILLE, 1883

Minerva Nichols watched as Emer rubbed her back. The poor girl was working too hard, especially for a seventeen-year-old. She should have some fun at her age. The linens she had scrubbed hung on the line. With the warm weather, they would be dry in no time and ready for ironing. She'd been right to take the girl in two years before when she'd arrived in Leadville, rather rough around the edges. With her looks and body, she could have made a lot of money working in one of the saloons. Minerva shuddered thinking just how close the girl had come.

If she hadn't stepped in, the innocent girl would have been destroyed. *Just like I was. If someone had stepped in to save me, what would my life have turned out like? Stop that, you've done well for yourself. Nobody associates you with the girl they knew as Lily Long Legs.*

Lewis Nichols had married her and taken her to Leadville, sure they would find riches in the mountains. And they had, more than they could have ever dreamed of. The recent silver strikes had brought the best and worst to their little town. Sudden wealth had a bad effect on people. She frowned, thinking of her own husband. Seemed he wouldn't be happy no matter how rich they became.

"What?"

Minerva blinked rapidly, her attention focused back on Emer. "Nothing, dear. I just thought you looked a little tired. You can't work day and night, Emer."

"I can and I will. I have to get to Boston." Emer wiped her forehead with her sleeve before brushing some dirt off her pants.

Minerva smiled. It had been her idea to let the girl continue to dress in pants and a shirt. It offered a little protection against the hazards of working in a town with so many single men. "I can buy you a ticket to Boston."

At the look on Emer's face, Minerva quickly continued. "It's a loan, not charity. You can pay me back when you find your sister."

"No, thank you."

"Emer, you are as ornery as a miner's mule. Giving

hard-working, honest men grubstakes is how my husband made his fortune. Why can't I grubstake you?'

"It's not the same and you know it. I don't have a claim on a mine. I ain't never going to hit gold or silver to pay you back."

"Please, Emer, let me help." Minerva loved the girl. She was like the daughter she would never have. Not now. It was too late.

"No, but thank you, Miss Minerva. You helped me enough already."

"Have it your way but will you at least move to Denver with me? I don't want to leave you here."

Sensing Emer was about to decline, Minerva spoke quickly. "Wait 'til you see the house Lewis bought. It's huge. I will need a lot of help setting it up. I know I can find domestics in Denver but it would be really helpful if I had someone I could trust." Minerva saw she wasn't winning any ground. It was time to play the guilt card. "You know those respectable people aren't going to take to me immediately. I need you. Please say you will, Emer."

Emer didn't reply but she seemed to be listening more openly now. She had to play on her sympathy.

"Things have been difficult lately. Lewis is away so much. You would be doing me a favor. Having a friendly face around means a lot."

"I can see why you are so successful, Miss Minerva. You could charm honey off a bee."

Minerva laughed before thoughts of her husband removed the smile from her face. There was a time when Lewis would do anything for her. Now, it seemed as if he couldn't bear to be in her company for five minutes. She looked down at her hands. She knew the respectable people in Denver would look down on her. She had worked the fields, did her own housework, cooked meals and worked behind a store counter. Heck, she had even ridden horseback transporting gold to Denver for the postal express. There was very little she hadn't done and some things she wasn't proud of. *Nobody in Denver knows of Lily Long Legs. You can leave her here in the mountains. Lewis is the only one who shares your secret. He's not likely to tell anyone.*

Lewis. Her heart twisted with longing. How she loved that man, but she'd lost him. She could see it in his eyes. Darn it, anyway. Her blood, sweat and tears had helped to secure his wealth. If she hadn't insisted on opening stores and using his early profits to buy their land, he would never have had the fifty dollars worth of tools and goods to grubstake the French miners. She had continued to run the store and restaurant with Emer's help despite the $250,000 her husband got from his investment in the Frenchmen.

Maybe that is why this girl had appealed to her so much. Emer reminded her of herself. Just like her, the girl had grown up in the wild west. She lived life on her wits. Minerva had probed but Emer refused to tell her why she had run away. Given the reasons she had left home all those years ago, she decided not to pry. Some hurts were better left in the past.

"Will you come to Denver, Emer?"

"Yes, Miss Minerva. I'll come but I can't stay long. I'm heading for Boston to find my sister just as soon as the warm weather comes along."

CHAPTER 6

BOSTON 1884

Emer got off the train and looked around the station. She was finally here. She hadn't meant to stay so long in Denver but Miss Minerva—Minnie, as she now called her—had needed her.

Her hands clenched as she remembered how quickly the joy of moving to the big house in Denver had soured. Mr. Nichols had no sooner arrived in the big city before he had taken to going out every night. Rumors of affairs and relationships abounded. His wealth grew at a phenomenal rate, not least due to his investment in other mines, banks and a couple of saloons. He wasn't fussy how he made his money.

Emer wasn't aware she was scowling as she thought of how Lewis had treated Minnie. It wasn't enough he had left her for another lady but he had also spread some malicious gossip about Miss Minerva's past. Emer had come across her mistress arguing with her husband. On hearing a loud slap, she had rushed into the room to find Miss Minerva on the floor, Lewis standing over her.

She couldn't believe how her friend and mentor had seemed to age overnight. "Miss Minerva. What have you done to her?" she'd shouted at Lewis, before rushing to help Miss Minerva to sit on the bed.

Lewis had smirked nastily. "Dear old Emer. Still calling my darling wife Miss Minerva. Isn't it about time you told the girl how you earned your first dollars? On your back?"

Emer had taken a step toward Lewis, her hand raised. He had retaliated by grabbing it and twisting it behind her back. She could still smell him as he'd pushed his body closer to hers, his face a hair's breath away from hers. "Careful, girl, or you may get a taste of the life your mistress used to lead. You are young enough yet." Emer had stamped on his toe and kicked him in the shin for good measure. If she'd had a gun, she would have shot him.

Men got away with murder. Patty's troubles had all involved men and now poor Minnie was the laughing stock of Denver. It didn't matter how rich she'd been. The respectable society she craved had immediately closed ranks on her. Lewis had divorced her and stolen all their investments. Minnie, as her mistress now preferred to be called, hadn't been able to fight back. She couldn't risk going to court and face more public condemnation.

Thankfully, she'd kept some investments hidden in her own name. She had bought lots of land and had stores in various towns. It was as if some instinct had told her Lewis would betray her.

Emer sighed. She missed Minnie already. She didn't care what her friend had done in her early life. She'd been good to her and protected her. Emer wiped a tear away. If it hadn't been for Minnie's kind heart, Emer may have ended up in one of Lewis's saloons, too.

Miss Minerva had taken a long trip overseas. Despite her husband's actions, Emer knew her friend prayed daily for her husband to admit he'd made a mistake and return to live with her. She couldn't imagine ever loving someone that much.

Lewis had made a complete fool of Minnie, yet she would have welcomed him back with open arms. Emer didn't think the man would ever come back. At least she hoped he wouldn't. If she ever set eyes on Lewis, she wouldn't be responsible for her actions.

Why was love so complicated? Emer believed it was overrated. She wasn't ever going to fall in love. It only caused problems. Emer gathered her bags together, ignoring the stares of the other passengers.

She was wearing her old uniform of pants and a shirt. Minnie had been appalled but Emer's reasoning that dressing like a boy would protect her had worked. Emer grinned. Minnie didn't know about the small pistol she had secured in her pocket. If any man tried his luck, he would be in for a surprise.

CHAPTER 7

Where did Ma say she'd lived when she was a kid? It was down near the docks. Might as well head there and see what she could find. The Catholic Church was a good place to look. Whatever else her ma may have kept hidden, she had never stopped talking about the church her mother had dragged her to every day and twice on a Sunday. She'd sworn it was the Church's fault she'd run from Boston. Emer guessed the real reason involved a man. Where Patty was involved, trouble always equaled a man.

Emer walked, her stomach grumbling with hunger. She didn't want to spend any more money. Minnie had been generous but Emer didn't know how long the money had to last. Her family would give her something to eat. They would be so pleased to see her. Ignoring the various street traders and intoxicating smells coming from the local cafés, she kept the church spire in sight.

Finally, she pushed the door open and stepped inside. Immediately, the smell of incense brought images of a previous visit to mind. She'd been a little girl. She remembered hiding behind her ma's skirts as music filled the building. Her ma had been crying but Emer couldn't remember why.

Looking around her, she spotted a priest kneeling near the altar. She decided to rest until he finished. It wouldn't be a good idea to annoy him by interrupting him. She needed his help. As she settled back on the bench, she let the peaceful atmosphere soak into her bones. You wouldn't know you were at the dockside. The air inside the church didn't stink of fish and there was only muffled noise coming from outside. She let her eyes close as she rested her weary legs.

A cough awakened her. Scrambling to stand up, she saw the priest standing in front of her.

"Sit down and rest a while, young man." The priest coughed. His gaze moving from her head to her toes and back again. "You're a girl. What are you doing dressed like that? Are you on your own?"

"I ain't—I mean, I haven't got anyone else, Father. It's just me."

"Are you in trouble? Hungry?"

Emer shook her head and nodded in response to his questions, causing him to laugh.

"If I can interpret, you are not in trouble, but you are hungry." The priest's eyes twinkled. "My name is Father Molloy. Why don't you come into my house and we will see what Mrs. Raines has to offer?"

"Father, could I ask you something first."

"By all means. Let me sit down, though. At my age, standing is a challenge."

Emer took a deep breath. Despite her shaking hands, her instincts told her the priest was a kind man. She could trust him. Not with the whole truth but with some of it.

"My ma told me, on her death bed, that she had a mother here in Boston. I came to find my granny and my sister. My sister's name is Sorcha Matthews." Emer guessed her sister would have the same surname. Ma hadn't married. "Do you know her, Father?"

Emer saw recognition dawn on his face but there was something else, too. Sadness or something else. She wasn't quite sure.

"Indeed, I do. She lived at the orphanage and I saw her at least once a week. But that was a while back."

In her excitement, Emer missed the fact the priest used the past tense.

"Can you point me in the direction and I will go see her now?" Emer stood, eager to finally meet the sister she hadn't known about.

"I'm sorry, child, but that's not possible. Sorcha doesn't live in the orphanage anymore."

"Well, where does she live then? I can get a cab, provided it's not too far away. I have money but I wouldn't want to waste it."

"Sorcha's married now and lives in Clover Springs. Colorado."

Emer sat back down with a bump. Colorado. Her sister had been in Colorado this whole time. How on earth was she going to find her sister now? She didn't have the money to go back to Colorado. *You would have if you had taken what Minnie wanted to give you.*

"Father, how long would it take to get to Clover Springs? Do I have to take a stage?" *Why you asking?* Emer pinched herself.

"It would only take a few days. Would you like me to write to Sorcha and tell her you intend visiting?"

"I'd like to surprise her."

"She is a married woman with young children. Her husband may prefer to know in advance the company his ten-year-old daughter will be mixing with."

"My sister has a ten-year old? Just how old is she?"

A smile creased Father Molloy's face. "She will soon be turning nineteen. Jenny is her stepdaughter." Father Molloy's stomach grumbled. "It's been a long time since breakfast. Why don't we go see what Mrs. Raines has put together for lunch?"

CHAPTER 8

Emer took a couple of seconds to consider her options. It wouldn't do any harm to have lunch with the priest. A free meal wasn't something she could pass up lightly, especially now when it looked like she would need to find a job. She followed Father Molloy out of the church and into his house. Enticing smells had them both sniffing the air appreciatively.

"Mrs. Raines is an amazing cook." Father Molloy patted his round belly. "Some may say too good."

Mrs. Raines stopped dead at the sight of Emer.

"What on earth?"

"Mrs. Raines, this is Emer Matthews."

"Emer, you're a girl. What are you dressed like a boy for? You in trouble? We don't need any trouble here."

Emer stared back at the other woman, whose disapproval was written all over her face.

Father Molloy coughed loudly. Emer watched the red stain move up the housekeeper's neck and into her face.

"What I meant to say was, you look hungry. Why don't you sit and eat?"

Emer put her bag at her side before taking a seat. They enjoyed an excellent lunch, despite the house-keeper's tutting and raised eyebrows.

Father Molloy told Emer a few stories about her granny. He also shared tidbits of information about Sorcha, her sister.

"She looks rather like you. Yes, the family resemblance is quite strong. No wonder I thought I had met you before."

Emer wished the priest had a picture. After they finished lunch, the priest suggested they retire to the sitting room to enjoy their coffee in comfort. Mrs. Raines fussed around the old man, insisting he put a rug over his legs and replace his shoes with slippers. After sitting for a while in companionable silence, Father Molloy sat up straighter.

"Why did you run away, Emer?"

"I didn't run, Father. I told you I had to come and find my sister."

"You could have written a letter. No. When you have been a priest for as long as I have, you develop a sixth sense. I can see you are in trouble or at least you were. So, please tell me, why did you run?"

"I had to, Father." Emer hoped her clipped tone would prevent him asking any further questions.

"Tell me, child. A trouble shared is a trouble halved."

"Patty—I mean, Ma—wanted me to live with this man. He wasn't a nice man. He wasn't decent or anything but he was powerful and dangerous. She was worried he'd do something to her if she didn't give me to him."

The frown on Father Molloy's face made him rather fierce looking.

"Give you? You are not an object for one person to play with."

"You try telling that to my Ma." Emer had to change the subject. She didn't know how the priest would react to knowing she had spent the last two years living with a fallen woman. Not much different to growing up with outlaws, she guessed. "She's good at giving away her kids. Apart from Sorcha, is there any more of us out there?"

"I don't know, Emer. I didn't know your ma but as I told you over lunch, I knew your grandmother very well. She was a fine, decent woman. Did her best for Sorcha. She kept her living with her for years. I think she thought Patricia might come back to claim her. She used to say she would when she was settled."

"Good job she died, then, as she would have been waiting forever."

"Emer." Father Molloy's tone held a hint of reproof. "You may not like her but she's still your ma. She did come back once. She spent a few days with your granny but then she went away again. I think she may have wanted to leave you here, but your granny was an old woman at that point. She couldn't handle another child."

"Nobody wanted me. That's the story of my life, Father. Emer forced herself to look out the window. She didn't like showing weakness to anyone, not even a priest.

"Sadie Matthews wasn't like that. She would have gone to the end of the earth for her family but as I said, she was old. She begged Patricia to give you to the nuns to take care of. She had a hope you and Sorcha might be adopted by the same family." Father Molloy sighed before taking a drink of his coffee. "Anyway, one day you were here staying with Sadie and the next you were gone. Broke Sadie's heart. She died not long after."

Emer's heart twisted for the grandmother she never knew. What would her life have been like if the woman had taken her in? Or Patty had given her to the orphanage? The dream of Sorcha being adopted didn't happen if her sister had been there until she was eighteen.

"Sorcha wasn't adopted."

"No. It wasn't possible as her mother was still alive."

"Was Sorcha happy with the nuns?"

A cloud flitted over the priest's face and he suddenly found the view outside the window very interesting. "Is that the time? We best find Mrs. Raines and get you settled for tonight. We will write to Sorcha tomorrow."

"Thank you, Father. You have been very kind."

The priest gave her arm a quick rub as he called for the housekeeper.

"I am not at all sure about letting you travel all that way on your own, though."

Emer pretended not to hear him. *Just you try and stop me, Father.*

CHAPTER 9

Lawrence Shipley kicked off his shoes before sinking into the cushions of the sofa. The butler poured a snifter for him. He needed it after the talk with his father. It had taken him ages to convince his father to let him go to Denver to set up the new branch of Shipley Bank.

Father had wanted Roger to go. Lawrence frowned. Father still believed his older brother had more experience, and being older and married meant he was more mature. What did being married have to do with setting up a bank? In Father's eyes, it meant Roger was more conservative and less likely to take risks.

He was a mature twenty-three-year-old. Sure, he liked to have fun. He had done everything his parents expected and more in the two years he had been forced to go work in the bank.

"Hello, darling. Why aren't you dressed for dinner?"

"Mother." Lawrence stood to kiss his mother on the cheek. When she sat down, he poured another drink before taking his seat.

"Isn't it rather early?"

"No, Mother." Lawrence drained the drink, ignoring the look his actions received.

"What are you sulking about now, Lawrence?"

"I am not sulking, Mother. I have had a long day."

"Did your Father agree to you going to Denver?"

"What do you know about that?"

"Lawrence, dear. Your father and I have been married a long time. There is very little I don't know about. Your boorish behavior would imply he decided not to send you."

"Oh, no, he's sending me all right."

"So why the long face? Isn't this what you said you wanted?"

"Yes, it is, but Father insisted Mitchell come, too."

"Ah."

"Exactly, Mother. Father obviously doesn't think I am up to the job. That's why he saddled me with ferret-face."

"Lawrence. Mitchell is a long-serving bank employee, not to mention a distant cousin. His knowledge and experience will assist you in Denver. It is not like Boston."

"It's hardly the Wild West, Mother. There are many banks in Denver and in surrounding areas. I have completed the two years experience in the Boston office under my darling brother's guidance." Lawrence tried to modulate his tone. Irritating his mother would only lead to more problems. "I met all of Father's requirements and now he saddles me with Mitchell. Well, I simply won't agree to it."

"Lawrence, for all your bluster about being an adult, you are very immature. Have I not told you over and over again, life is a series of battles? There are some you must win and there are those you don't enter into at all." His mother took a dainty sip of her drink before continuing. "Mitchell is part of the package. Going to Denver or not is your choice but Mitchell goes regardless."

Lawrence couldn't help but be impressed. Behind his mother's flawless beauty was a rock solid business mind. If she'd been born a man, she could run for president. *Perish the thought.* Mother in charge of the country didn't bear thinking about.

"Now, go get dressed for dinner. The Histons are coming. You remember their daughter, Alicia. Such a charming girl and wealthy in her own right."

"Don't start that again, Mother."

"I am simply stating a fact. Alicia Histon is a beautiful, talented, wealthy young lady. A perfect asset for a vice president of Shipley Bank."

"Marry her to Mitchell, then. She'd appeal to him. He hasn't a mind of his own, either."

Lawrence watched his mother's reaction closely. She was quick to hide the glint of amusement behind her usual mask. "Mitchell's future is none of my concern. Robert is already married so I get to put my undivided attention into finding you a suitable companion."

Lawrence groaned. "Mother, really. Do you have to sound so clinical? Where's your romance? What about marrying for love?"

"Love is for peasants. I barely knew your father before we got married and we have a good relationship."

Lawrence winced. His parents weren't close. They put on a performance whenever they had guests, but in reality, they spent little time together. Father preferred other, younger female company. He wasn't sure whether Mother knew or not. He wasn't going to be the one to enlighten her. It didn't do to get on the wrong side of his mother.

"You have a duty to this family, Lawrence." His mother's tone held more than a trace of steel. "Never forget who holds the purse strings." Once more the mask descended and his mother turned back into the social butterfly. "Now, try not to be late. We do not want to keep Alicia and her parents waiting."

* * *

DINNER WAS A TORTUROUS AFFAIR. As he'd suspected, Alicia seemed incapable of having an intelligent conversation. Sure, she was pretty but his sister's dolls had more life.

His mother hinted, more than once, he should take her for a walk around the gardens, staying within sight of the balcony window. Finally, he bowed to the less than subtle hints. Taking Alicia by the arm, he walked her around the gardens, trying his best to look interested in her chatter. Alicia talked about the flowers but he didn't listen after the first few minutes. He pandered to her for a while but couldn't restrain a yawn of boredom. She had fled back to her parents in tears, getting him a dressing down from his mother, along with another lecture on his duty to his family. *Duty and banking. There had to be more to life.*

CHAPTER 10

Emer knocked at the door. Mrs. Raines opened it and escorted her into the front parlor. "Father Molloy will be with you shortly. Would you like tea while you wait?"

"No, thank you, Mrs. Raines."

Emer sat in the slightly shabby room looking around her. She was tired, having spent the last few days trying to find work. She hated wearing dresses but Mrs. Raines had insisted. It wasn't decent for a young lady to be wearing pants.

Harvey had been right. There wasn't much call for a girl like her in Boston. She didn't think to get a reference from Minnie before she left on her travels. The cafes and hotels she had tried didn't believe she had experience. There seemed to be thousands of others looking for work. At this rate, she would never get to Clover Springs. The cost of the train ticket was way beyond her budget.

She needed a miracle.

The door opened and Father Molloy came in, his face creased in a smile.

"Good morning, Emer. How are you this fine day?"

Emer couldn't answer. She didn't want to disappoint him. He seemed so happy.

"Have you found a job yet?"

"No, Father. There are some opportunities I have yet to explore."

"That's wonderful."

"What?" Emer wondered if the priest was drunk but there was no smell of alcohol.

"I've been offered a fantastic opportunity. I told Katie I would see her again."

Katie? Who was she? Maybe she should call Mrs. Raines.

"Of course, I forgot. You won't know who Katie is or Mary for that matter. But you will soon enough. I am going to Clover Springs and taking you with me."

Emer couldn't speak but simply stared at the priest.

"Cat got your tongue? Did you hear what I said? I thought you wanted to meet your sister."

"I do, Father, but I don't understand. How? When?"

"I ran into an old parishioner. I wasn't always parish priest in this district. I have some very wealthy parishioners and one of them is traveling to Denver.

They have offered to let us join them in their private car."

Emer's excitement vanished. She had seen first-hand what wealthy people did to those who didn't fit in their circles. "Charity, you mean."

"An act of kindness, my dear Miss Matthews. One neither of us can afford to turn down." Father Molloy's tone irritated Emer. She wasn't a child.

"Father, you take their charity. I can't. I don't have any suitable clothes to wear to be traveling with rich folks." Emer stood. "I will be on my way. Tell Sorcha I will see her sometime."

"Emer Matthews, sit back down. Some day we will discuss the sin of pride. The Shipleys are one of the most prominent families in Boston. They will have their own private car on that train." Father Molloy lowered his voice, softening his tone at the same time. "Did your ma never tell you not to look a gift horse in the mouth? I can't tell you how long I have wanted to go check up on my girls."

"Katie and Mary?"

"Yes, both young girls much like yourself when they first left Boston to travel to Colorado. They became mail order brides, just like Sorcha did. All three of them married fine men from what Katie Sullivan tells me in her letters. I would like to meet these men for myself. I would also like to cuddle Ella,

Katie's darling little daughter. Although to be fair, I am not at all certain she is a darling."

Emer let the priest ramble on. She had prayed for a miracle and here it was. She could go to Clover Springs and find her sister. And it wouldn't cost her anything. *Only your pride.*

CHAPTER 11

CLOVER SPRINGS

Sorcha rubbed the clothes with soap. Her fingers hurt at the friction but the pain didn't stop her thoughts from wandering. What would her sister be like? Would she bring their ma with her? What would they think of her? Brian? The girls?

She took her frustration out on the clothes, her actions splashing water over everything in a wide radius. Why did her sister have to make an appearance now? All her life, she had wanted a family. Now she had one. Life was good and yet something was missing. Her sister was her blood. She was also a stranger.

"What did my brother do to get you so worked up?"

"Nandita. You're back. I thought you would be away longer." Sorcha let the clothes fall back into the tub as she rushed to give her sister-in-law a hug. "Where are the children?"

"Playing with the girls. See?" Nandita pointed to where the children were playing in the meadow. "So why are you in such a temper?"

"I was thinking about my sister."

"Have you had another letter? You seemed excited the last time when you told Katie and Mary. What's changed?"

Sorcha picked up one of Brian's shirts. It smelled of sweat and horses but still she hugged it close. It was comforting.

"What if she doesn't like me?"

Nandita laughed loudly. "Sorcha Petersen, everyone loves you. You make us feel better."

Sorcha put the shirt into the water. She needed to change the subject. "What has Chief Running Buffalo decided?"

Nandita frowned. "He says the time has come to join the reservation in Montana."

The clothes were once more forgotten as Sorcha enveloped Nandita in a rather wet hug.

"Chief Running Buffalo has had enough. He knows his luck isn't going to last. He cannot keep outwitting the soldiers. The tribe is hungry and lonely for other family members already living in Montana."

"When will he go?"

"Winter is coming. They need to move soon if they want to be on the reservation before the worst of the weather hits."

"What are you going to do?"

Nandita's gaze moved toward where Brian and Frank were working.

"I do not know yet."

"You have to speak to Frank."

Nandita tore her eyes away from the man she loved to look at Sorcha. "How can I? He hasn't said anything yet."

"He loves you, you know he does."

"I do not know that, Sorcha, and neither do you." Nandita stood straighter. "Let me help you with those clothes. The sun will not shine all day."

Sorcha knew better than to try to convince Nandita to speak to Frank. Her friend was stubborn and proud.

* * *

AFTER NANDITA HUNG the clothes on the line, she wandered closer to her brother's work area. She watched as Frank worked, his focus totally centered on the job in hand. His ebony skin glistened with sweat, and every so often he brushed his muscular arm across his forehead.

He stoked the fire, the heat radiating to where she was standing. How could he bear working near the inferno for hours at a time?

He wore a thin black leather vest over his chest for protection rather than modesty. His arms and hands bore traces of scars, but not as bad as the ones on his back. She could still feel the groves in his skin from where he had been whipped as a child. Hungry, he had taken some food from his master's plate. The overseer had spotted Frank sharing the scraps with some of the other slave children and decided he had to be punished. He had left the child scarred for life.

Nandita wrapped her arms around herself. She wanted so much to make a life with this man. They had shared more than a few stolen kisses. She smiled, thinking of the night they had swam in the river. She'd been bathing while Little Beaver kept watch. Her step-son, distracted by an animal, had run off to hunt leaving her alone.

Hearing noises, she had turned to find Frank standing on the shore. She had seen the look on his face. Keeping his eyes on hers, he had jumped into the river to join her.

They had swum around for a while before he took her in his arms and kissed her. She moved out of his embrace, her fingertips tracing her lips. She had never been kissed like that before. She liked it.

Nandita opened her eyes. That first kiss had been months ago, not long after Sorcha had first arrived in Clover Springs. Although she believed she was divorced, Sleeping Bear had been the barrier stopping her from getting involved with Frank.

Sleeping Bear was dead now. They could be together. Just like they wanted. Only it wasn't that easy. Stay here with Frank and lose her Indian family or go with them and lose the man she loved.

As she watched Frank work, she wondered what life on a reservation would be like. She had heard Montana had more snow and less sun but she hadn't met anyone who lived there. So that might not be true.

What was true was she would have to say goodbye to her brother, Sorcha and their girls. She would miss them and her friends in Clover Springs. She couldn't imagine not being able to go anywhere she wished. She didn't know if one could get permission to leave the reservation.

Frank had already changed his whole life. He had left his home in the South to move to Colorado. She could understand him not wanting to move again. He had a good business here with Brian. Her brother, while skilled, didn't share Frank's expertise when it came to blacksmithing. He could shoe a horse but he preferred to concentrate on healing and training the animals.

She took a deep breath as he moved closer to the fire. She didn't want to distract him. His job was dangerous enough. Using his tongs, he removed a piece of red hot metal from the flames. He placed it on his anvil before bringing the hammer down to mold the piece into the shape he needed. Frank cared deeply for the horses he tended and every shoe fit as perfectly as he could make it.

Her thoughts wandered as he worked. The hissing of the water on the metal startled her.

"You going to stand there all day?"

Nandita gulped. How long had he known she was watching him?

"I, um—Sorcha wondered if you were staying for dinner?"

"You going?"

Nandita flushed as he waited for an answer. His deep brown eyes held hers.

"Yes."

"Good. After dinner, we will take a walk. Just the two of us."

Nandita nodded. He didn't smile. Instead, his chocolate eyes glowed as they raked her from head to foot.

"Please ask Sorcha if she needs anything mended. She can leave it here." He pointed to the shelf. "I will see you later."

He turned back to his work, leaving her with no option but to walk back to the house. She was torn between being excited at the thought of spending some time alone with him and the fact that this could be one of the last times they saw one another.

CHAPTER 12

CLOVER SPRINGS

Dinner was a lively affair. The girls fought over who would sit beside Nandita so she settled herself between the two of them.

"Did you know Ben is having a baby?" Meggie asked Nandita.

"Mary is having the baby, silly. Boys don't have babies."

"Jenny, don't call your sister silly," Sorcha admonished her stepdaughter. "It's wonderful news. Mary is so excited although Davy is annoying her. He keeps insisting she stay home and rest."

Nandita put a smile on her face as she pretended to be surprised at the news. She had guessed some time ago. It wasn't hard, given Mary had been sick every morning.

She was happy for Mary, who had been a good

friend to her and her children. But it was impossible to feel happy when her own life was about to be torn apart.

Sorcha had prepared a wonderful meal but it might as well have been rocks for all Nandita tasted. She could feel Frank's eyes on her but when she caught his gaze, he looked away. What was he thinking?

Surely, he knew how she felt about him. She couldn't tell him. Well, not in plain language, yet all her little hints seem to have been wasted. *What did you expect? He isn't Indian so he isn't familiar with the ways of your people.* She picked at her food. Sorcha glanced at her a couple of times, a question in her eyes, but Nandita ignored her.

She couldn't help thinking her life as she knew it was over. It was time she made a decision. Standing, she excused herself. "Thank you for the lovely meal, Sorcha. I will speak to you tomorrow." She risked a last look at Frank but he was staring at his plate. Putting a hand to her mouth, she ran from the house.

"BRIAN, I need to speak with you." Frank held his hands by his side, his back straight. "Can we go outside? Sorcha, thank you for the lovely meal and thank you, girls, for your beautiful company."

Meggie and Jenny giggled in response to Frank's

teasing. Frank glanced at Sorcha. She had a secretive smile on her face but she didn't say a word.

He walked back and forth outside the barn. It seemed to take Brian an hour to follow him, when in reality it was only seconds.

"What's up with you? I would say you were pale with fright but that's a bit difficult given your coloring."

Frank didn't laugh although he would usually have done. He admired Brian so much, not just for his skill with horses but for the unquestioning friendship he had extended. He wasn't a man to judge someone by how they looked, hence his jokes about his skin weren't offensive.

His silence was giving Brian cause for concern but he couldn't speak until his knees stopped trembling. He hoped his friend and boss couldn't see just how nervous he was.

"I want to marry Nandita."

"I know that."

Frank's head shot up. "You know? How could you? I haven't told anyone."

Brian laughed softly. "You didn't have to say anything. Your eyes and actions told everyone."

"You mean... what do you mean everyone?" Frank swallowed hard. "Does she know?"

"If, by she, you mean my sister, I assume she does,

although we have never discussed it. Why don't you ask her?"

"I would but I wasn't sure how. Don't I have to go to speak to the chief or do I speak to you? I would speak to her father but..." Frank wiped his hands on his trousers. "Help me, Brian. It is not something I am used to doing."

"I should hope not. I know the Indian way is to take many wives but my sister is half white."

"Do you think I am not good enough for her?"

"What? No, of course not." Brian laughed at Frank's scowl. "Sorry, that came out wrong. Of course you are good enough. I can't think of anyone I would rather have as a brother-in-law."

Frank let his shoulders relax. Brian wasn't good with words and it wasn't unusual for his boss to say something the wrong way.

"What I meant, Frank, was my sister deserves to be the only wife. You never mentioned your family. I assume you haven't been married."

"No. I ain't had the time to go courting. But I've been saving hard and have my own place now. It's not as big as this but you know that. I have good skills and business is expanding all the time."

"So why haven't you asked her?"

Frank looked away. He hated having to admit he was scared. He thought it was bad when he'd run away from his master during the war but this was worse.

Facing Nandita, telling her how he felt about her, it was just about the hardest thing he ever had to do.

"Frank, I would be honored to have you as a member of our family. Go speak to my sister before you lose your nerve again." Brian clapped Frank so hard on the back, he nearly stumbled.

CHAPTER 13

He walked slowly in the direction of the creek where Nandita was waiting.

He knew she heard him approach, despite him being careful not to step on any twigs. You couldn't surprise an Indian. They had been too well trained in learning about their environment from an early age. Nandita stared into the water, her waist-length black hair glistening in the moonlight.

"Nan, I'm sorry I kept you waiting."

She didn't respond.

"I didn't follow you as I wanted to speak to Brian."

"So speaking to my brother is more interesting than going for a walk with me?" She turned to him, her face twisted into a fierce expression. He reached for her but she moved out of his range.

"Nan, don't be angry. I have something to say."

"To me or would you like me to bring my brother?"

"Nandita, you listen to me now. I have had enough of your tantrums. Be a good wife and listen."

"Wife? I am not your wife."

"Not yet. But I would like you to be. Heck, Nandita, this isn't the way it should be." Frank moved closer to her, relieved she stood still. He didn't rate his chances of catching her should she decide to run.

He pushed a strand of her silky hair back from her face. Still she didn't react but stood like a statue, her eyes glued to his. Putting his hands on either side of her face, he took the last step to close the distance between them. "Nandita, will you do me the honor of becoming my wife?"

He didn't give her a chance to say anything but dipped his head to leave a fleeting kiss on her lips.

* * *

Moving fully into his arms, she raised her face for another one.

"Is that a ..."

Her kiss stopped him from finishing his question. Their lips moved slowly at first before deepening into a tender embrace. Her legs felt weak but in a good way. She liked how her blood raced to different parts of her body.

She leaned against him, not wanting to break this

moment. After a couple of minutes, he groaned as he pushed her aside. She tried to move back closer to him but he stopped her.

"Nandita, I can't. I won't be able to stop."

She didn't care. She tried to bring his face closer for another kiss but he kept her at arm's length.

"Nandita, stop. Please." He kissed her lightly on the forehead before pulling her close to him. "You didn't answer the question."

"Yes, I want to marry you," she whispered, "but I can't."

His obvious delight at her first words disappeared. "Why? Sleeping Bear is dead. You are free. Aren't you?"

Nandita moved away from him, wrapping her arms around her body. "I have no husband, true, but what of my family? If I marry you, I will lose them."

He moved to her, putting a hand on her shoulder. When she didn't pull away, he pulled her gently into his arms. "You cannot go live on the reservation. You will be like a caged bird. Your heart will break and you will die." At her sob, he pulled her closer, kissing the top of her head. "Stay here, be my wife. You will be free."

"You don't understand."

Her words cut him to the bone. Pushing her away, he walked to the water's edge, trying to stop the memories her words had unleashed from flooding his brain. "I do not understand? How could you say that to me? I know what it is like not to be free. To see your father and mother auctioned off like cattle. To watch your family moved from place to place in ankle irons."

He whirled back to face her.

"Never tell me again I do not understand what it is to be a captive. But the difference is, I chose to be free. You are free yet you are choosing to be a slave."

Frank marched away. He knew he hadn't been totally fair. But he couldn't deal with anyone now. He knew tonight the nightmares would be worse than usual. Tears flowed unchecked down his cheeks as he made his way via the river bed to the place he called home.

Nandita stared after Frank, her fingernails pinching the palms of her hands. Of course he understood what it was like not to be free. How could she have hurt the man she loved so badly? She'd seen the scars caused by his childhood, not just the physical ones on his back but the ones that kept him awake at night. She fell to her knees as her emotions overcame her. She cried until there were no tears left. Lying by the river, she stared into the water. *Great Spirit, help me. Please, help me.*

BRIAN WAITED for Nandita and Frank to come back but neither arrived.

"Sorcha, if something happened, they would have come back to tell us."

"Maybe they wanted some time alone. It's so romantic. Finally, they are going to get married. I mean, they have been in love for ages."

Brian smiled at the woman in his arms. He had nearly lost her through fear. She was right. He had to trust the feelings his sister and friend had for one another. But it didn't stop the ice forming in the pit of this stomach. He couldn't shake the feeling something was wrong. Sorcha reached up to pull him toward her. One kiss and everything else was forgotten.

CHAPTER 14

BOSTON 1884

Lawrence stifled a grin. It had been a while since his mother had been in such a flap.

"Yes, dear," his father said over the top of his newspaper.

"Don't 'yes, dear' me. It's all your fault. You were the one who said we were opening a branch in Denver."

Lawrence's father threw his eyes up to heaven behind cover of the newspaper. Lawrence held his napkin over his mouth to hide his grin. Only when fully composed did he address his mother.

"Mother, whatever is the matter?"

"You can stop pretending innocence. You know what happened. Your father invited Father Molloy and one of his, his…"

"Parishioners, dear."

His mother threw a killer look at his father, who was once more hidden behind his newspaper.

"Father Molloy and one of his young charges, a girl, to accompany us on our trip to Denver. They will share our car." His mother stopped talking to take a bite of her buttered roll. "Why couldn't you just buy them the train tickets, Roland?"

"Our trip?" Lawrence nearly choked on his coffee. "You said Mitchell was coming but I didn't know you intended on traveling, too, Mother."

"Of course I am coming. I am not about to let the two of you manage social events surrounding the opening of the branch. Neither of you are exactly socially aware."

Lawrence tried hard to control his temper. His mother seemed to think he was a child, and an incapable one at that. "Mother, I think both of us are quite capable of attending a dinner after the grand opening. It seems silly to drag you all the way out West."

"I am going, Lawrence, and that is the end of the matter." His mother's frosty tone could have chilled champagne.

Lawrence exchanged another look with his father but neither said anything. His mother's moods were legendary but this latest seemed to be worse than all the previous ones combined.

"I will invite Father Molloy for afternoon tea

tomorrow. Lawrence, you will be busy at the office, as will you, Roland."

Lawrence hid behind his napkin again. His mother didn't want an audience. He couldn't wait to meet the girl who had put his mother on edge.

* * *

EMER TRIED to quell her panic as the cab drove through the gated entrance and up the long circular driveway. Looking out the window, she saw the grandest house she had ever seen. Minnie's mansion was small in comparison. The cab stopped in front of the wide steps in the middle of two thick white columns. She stepped down from the cab carefully while Father Molloy paid the driver.

"Father, please, let me leave now. I don't belong here."

"Emer, we've discussed this. Mrs. Shipley invited us for afternoon tea. Now, hold your head up high and take my arm. We are going in."

Emer took his arm and promptly tripped over her skirt. She would have fallen if the old priest hadn't helped her. The manservant opened the front door. Emer stared as they walked into the wide hallway, her shoes making loud noises on the marble floors. Up ahead, she saw a large curved staircase. *Wonder what the upstairs looks like?*

The butler showed them into a spacious room, advising them Mrs. Shipley would be right with them. Emer walked over to the patterned walls. The room was so pretty. Heavy curtains were tied at the sides of the large windows, allowing light to flood the room. The door opened again to admit a tall, striking woman. She watched as their hostess greeted Father Molloy warmly.

"Sit down, please, Father Molloy. Tea will be served in a few minutes."

Father Molloy shook the lady's hand before turning to Emer. "My dear Mrs. Shipley, let me present Miss Emer Matthews."

Emer bobbed, keeping her hands behind her back. The lady nodded but Emer didn't miss the cold stare raking her over. The chills raced down her spine as she was obviously found wanting.

"I am so glad you decided to take Roland up on his offer. Traveling can be such a tedious affair, don't you think?"

"It's been a long time since I traveled further than the parish boundaries. I am rather excited." The priest's joy was obvious.

"What takes you to Colorado? Surely the Church isn't moving you there after all these years?"

The butler arrived with the tea, interrupting the flow of conversation. Emer caught the servant looking at her with the same disdainful glance his mistress had used. Making sure Father Molloy wasn't watching, she stuck her tongue out at the butler as he was leaving the room.

"Not at all. This is a vacation. I wish to visit with some of the girls who left us a few years back. They have settled in a small town in Colorado. Clover Springs."

"Don't think I have been there, Father."

Doesn't look like you would like to go, either.

"Ah, Lawrence, thank you for joining us. I thought you would be too busy."

Emer stifled a giggle as the woman's tone suggested she was chastising a school boy rather than a grown man. *What you mean was you wanted him to stay away.* She was curious to meet the son of this old witch. She looked up to find laughing green eyes staring back at her. *How long had he been standing there? Did he see me stick out my tongue at the butler?* She sat straighter, instinctively drawn to the young man. He was everything his mother wasn't. His smile was genuine. It didn't hurt he was attractive. Not classically good looking but what was the word? Distinguished. *You mean rich.*

"Ahem. Nice to meet you, Miss Matthews."

How long had he been standing in front of her? Emer recovered quickly. "You, too, Mr. Shipley." She tried to take her hand back but he held onto it for a few seconds.

Emer almost fell back into the seat when he let her hand go. She caught the amusement in his eyes.

"Mother, would you like me to pour?"

The conversation continued between Father Molloy and their host but Emer wasn't listening. She couldn't. She could feel him sitting beside her, scrutinizing her. Unlike the servants and his mother, he didn't seem to be repulsed, though. He seemed—well, almost interested.

"Have you lived in Boston long, Miss Matthews?"

Why did he have to ask me a question just as I took a bite of cake? She tried to swallow the piece quickly but it went down the wrong way, resulting in a coughing fit. Mortified, she took the glass of water he offered, his mother's gaze drilling through both of them. Would this tea party ever end?

"Miss Matthews, perhaps you would like to go shopping before our trip?" Emer looked down at her dress, it hadn't looked too bad in Father Molloy's house but here, it was horrendous. "Colorado can be quite cold at this time of year. You will need some suitable outfits."

How am I going to pay for them, Duchess?

She almost choked again, fearing she had spoken out loud, as Mrs. Shipley continued. "I would accompany you myself but I have so many things going on before we leave. I will ask Kirsten, my ladies' maid, to go with you. She knows what to buy."

Emer found her voice. "Thank you very much, Mrs. Shipley, but there is no need…"

"There is every need." Mrs. Shipley's tone, although civil, held a ring of steel. "Kirsten will charge the purchases to my account. Oh, is that the time?" Mrs. Shipley stood, causing both men to stand also. "Please forgive me, Father Molloy, but Roland was invited to the governor's house this evening. I must start getting ready."

Father Molloy finished his tea hurriedly. "Thank you very much for your hospitality and kindness, Mrs. Shipley. Nice to see you again, Lawrence."

"You too, Father." Lawrence turned to Emer. Taking her hand, he leaned closer ,whispering, "Meeting you was the highlight of the afternoon. Don't let mother intimidate you. She is all front."

Emer didn't respond. She couldn't.

CHAPTER 15

Father Molloy insisted Emer come back to the house to show him her purchases. He had fallen down the stairs and twisted his ankle. He was stuck sitting on the sofa all day long. It was torture for such a sociable man. His parishioners were very kind but most of them had jobs and couldn't keep him company all day long.

Emer sat, hoping her stomach wouldn't start rumbling. The shopping trip had been everything she dreaded. Kirsten was almost as cold as her mistress, making it clear at every opportunity how much charity Mrs. Shipley was giving her.

"Do I have to travel with the Shipleys?" Emer asked the priest, keeping her fingers crossed hoping he would say no.

"Dorothea Shipley has been very kind to you,

Emer. The family is one of the most upstanding families in Boston."

"By upstanding, I guess you mean wealthy. Funny how money always brings respectability, isn't it?" Thinking of Lewis, Minnie's ex-husband, made her tone harder than she had intended.

"Don't mock me, Emer. I am not your enemy."

Emer looked at the ground, her stomach clenching. She hadn't meant to hurt the priest's feelings. He had been nothing but kind to her.

"Sorry, Father. I wish you were coming with me." Emer looked over at the man just in time to see the pain on his face. "I'm sorry. Sometimes the words just come out of my mouth so fast, I can't stop them."

"I know that, child. I may be a priest but I am also a man with failings. I admit to being very disappointed I won't be traveling with you. I so wanted to see my girls again."

"Maybe I could stay here and wait for you to recover. Doc said with rest, your leg should be better in a month or so."

"No, child. You must travel now."

The priest's tone told her he didn't want her to argue. But she did anyway.

"I don't want to travel with strangers, especially when they make it obvious they don't approve of me."

"Emer, there is prejudice everywhere. For example, you are judging the Shipleys because they are wealthy.

Just because someone has money doesn't mean that they are happy."

"Well, I guess so but Mrs. Shipley doesn't look at you as if you were something that smelled." Emer looked at the priest when he made a funny sound like a laugh but he recovered quickly.

"Why don't you go try on another one of those dresses she bought for you? I would never have thought about how uncomfortable you would have felt not having the right clothes to travel in. She is a very kind lady."

Kind, my foot. The lady was as low as a rattlesnake. Emer cringed remembering the venom in Mrs. Shipley's face when they had spoken earlier that day. The woman had left Emer with no doubt she considered her an imposition. She was only taking her along to keep up appearances.

Emer changed as Father Molloy had told her to. She touched the material gingerly. She had never owned something so fragile or fine in her whole life. She looked at her reflection. *I look like a real lady. Will Sorcha be impressed?*

She ran back into where Father Molloy waited. "Walk, child. Ladies don't run."

She turned around so he could get the full view of her dress. "Isn't it gorgeous, Father? I've never owned anything so pretty."

"You look beautiful, Emer, but remember true

beauty is on the inside."

"Yes, Father."

"Run along now, dear. Mrs. Raines has made you something to eat. I'm not hungry, although I am rather tired." The priest settled back on the sofa and closed his eyes. Emer looked at the old man as he slept. His leg must be more painful than he was willing to admit.

Emer had become very fond of Mrs. Raines. After witnessing her table manners, Mrs. Raines took Emer under her wing. She showed her how to eat properly, in particular the different types of cutlery to use.

The housekeeper patiently showed Emer how to act more like a lady. "Where did Father Molloy find you? I could lay a wager you didn't have any female role models, did you?"

Emer sat silently at the kitchen table.

"You can't just pick up food with your fingers. And close your mouth while you're eating." Emer picked up a fork but put it down again as a frown appeared on the housekeeper's face. "What about grace? You got to say thanks for the meal you are eating."

"I'm not eating. You keep lecturing me and me stomach thinks me throat's been cut."

"Emer Matthews. Curb your tongue. You can't use language like that. It isn't ladylike." The housekeeper went about the kitchen, muttering loud enough for Emer to hear. "Why is it down to me to change her into something resembling a lady? I've known Father

Molloy for a long time and seen many of his hare-brained schemes but this is the best one yet."

"That's better, Emer. Sit up straight and look that Shipley woman in the eye. She may have more money and have all the trappings that brings with it. In the eyes of God, you are just as good as she is, and don't you forget it."

CHAPTER 16

Time flew by and all too soon, Emer was standing on the station platform saying goodbye to Father Molloy. He had insisted on accompanying her to the station. Secretly, she was relieved. She dreaded the trip. The only saving grace was the thought of finally meeting her sister. Mrs. Shipley assured Father Molloy they would look after Emer. *I can look after myself. I've been doing it for years.* But she kept her mouth shut. The priest wasn't recovering as quickly as he should. It wouldn't be fair to add more drama to his life than she already had.

The whistle blew and Emer found herself fighting tears as she waved goodbye to the priest. She wasn't going to show weakness, not now. Sharing a railway car with the Shipley family would be a challenge. Mr. Shipley stayed in Boston but Mrs. Shipley, Lawrence and his awful cousin, Mitchell, were enough company for Emer.

The hours dragged by. Emer fidgeted, wishing more than once she had disobeyed Father Molloy and traveled with the servants. Then she could have worn her pants and shirt. She pulled at the collar of her dress. There was so much material, she felt suffocated. Moving was a problem, too, as she hadn't quite mastered walking like a lady. Every time she had to leave the car, she tripped, much to the amusement of Lawrence.

She had caught him looking at her a few times, his head slightly tilted to one side. Studying her, almost. As if she was something foreign. She didn't like how it made her feel. She tried staring him down but that only seemed to add to his amusement.

Emer twisted and turned in the bed. It was comfortable, certainly better than sleeping on a chair the whole trip. It wasn't the accommodation stopping her from sleeping. Every time she closed her eyes, she kept seeing his face, his green eyes dancing with merriment. Usually at something she did.

Like earlier that day, he had offered her the paper to read. She'd made the mistake of taking it and pretending to be engrossed in the content. He'd asked her over dinner what she had thought of some article. She'd made an excuse but she wasn't sure if he believed her. She wasn't about to admit she couldn't read properly. There wasn't much time for Patty to teach her things like that. Patty wasn't keen on sending her to school, either. Minnie had tried to make her pay more attention to her lessons but she hadn't. She couldn't help wishing she had.

"Good morning, Miss Matthews. Did you sleep well?"

Why did he always speak to her just as she took a bite of food? She chewed quickly, managing this time not to make a complete fool of herself.

"Yes, thank you. Did you?"

"Didn't sleep a wink. I hate traveling, don't you?"

She couldn't believe he was complaining when they were traveling in style compared to some. He only had to take a walk through the train to see what ordinary people had to put up with. He was typical of the class he belonged to. Rich, spoiled and so very attractive. Annoyed with herself, she took her temper out on him.

"You should try traveling without the benefit of the sleeping car. Then you would have something to grumble about."

Lawrence laughed heartily, surprising her. She hadn't meant it as a joke. She hated when rich people complained about suffering. If it had been Mitchell who had reacted this way, she'd have given him a lecture but Lawrence was different. Why? He's a spoiled rich man out for some fun to pass the time.

* * *

LAWRENCE'S STOMACH ached from laughing. He deliberately said things to Miss Matthews to upset her. Not in a bad way but just because he wanted to see her eyes sparkle. She wasn't beautiful in the way the debutantes he was used to were. Her hands weren't as soft, her skin showed signs of sun exposure and she walked like a man. *Some man—she's all woman and you know it.* Her face was one of the most expressive he had ever seen, possibly as she had never been coached to guard her emotions. With her, there was no secret code, no silly games. What you saw was what you got. At first, the change had been refreshing. Something to help pass the time until they arrived in Denver. But now?

He found himself seeking her out more often. She amused him but he wasn't laughing at her, but with her. She was funny without being mean. He regretted embarrassing her yesterday with the newspaper. It was obvious she couldn't read, not least because she had held it upside down.

"Why are you so intent on going to Clover Springs, Miss Matthews?"

"I want to find my sister." Emer closed her mouth, her tone telling him the subject was closed. But he wanted to know more.

"Find your sister? Did you not grow up together?"

"No, we didn't. Circumstances kept us apart. That

is all I am going to say, Mr. Shipley. Your mother has already asked me loads of questions."

He hid a smile as her nose rose up when speaking of his mother. These two women were similar in so many ways—not that they would ever admit it.

"Have you ever been to Denver?"

"I lived there for a time." She looked down at her plate. Quite obviously, she didn't want to discuss it further but his curiosity was piqued.

"Really, where? Perhaps I know the people you stayed with?"

The glare she sent him told him to be careful. "That is not very likely, is it? Mr. Shipley, I am going to be frank. I cannot work out whether you are trying to be nice or you are simply passing time. Either way, this… conversation is boring. If you will excuse me, I wish to go for a walk."

When he stood, she turned her head slightly.

"Alone." With that, she walked off, leaving him speechless.

He watched her walk, unsteadily, out of the car. She was intriguing. There was no doubt about that. The more she tried to shut him out, the more he found himself wanting to get to know her. He loved the way she talked. She bit her nails when nervous and often stopped before continuing a sentence. A couple of times, he thought she had uttered a mild curse word. He sensed she was lonely, despite the brave front she put on. He had watched her, while pretending to read a book. When she let her guard down, he saw deep pain in her eyes. Someone had hurt her badly. His hands balled as he thought of anyone laying a finger on her. What was wrong with him? He barely knew the girl yet she brought out a protective side to him he never knew existed.

HER LEGS WERE SHAKING SO MUCH, Emer struggled to walk out of the dining car without losing her footing. What was Lawrence Shipley up to? Mitchell had already tried to find out details of her background, as had Mrs. Shipley. She hadn't told them anything. Now Lawrence was asking questions she didn't want to answer. Had Mrs. Shipley sent him or was he really interested? *Of course, he's not interested. He could have his pick of the ladies.*

Emer kept walking, wishing they were anywhere but on a train. There was a limit to how far she could go. On impulse, she decided to visit some of the other cars, hoping to find someone like her. Maybe a conversation with her own people would make the time pass faster.

She entered a car and smiled at a couple of ladies who seemed to be traveling alone. They looked like servant girls or maybe mail order brides like the ones

Father Molloy had sent. She asked one girl if she minded if she took a seat.

"Not at all, Miss. Would you like me to fetch your husband?"

Emer looked over her shoulder, wondering who the girl was speaking to before she realized it was her. "My husband..."

"You seem to be unwell, Miss. I seen you earlier with a nice gentleman. Should I fetch him?"

"No, please don't. I would just like to sit a while and talk."

The girls exchanged a look, leaving Emer feeling more uncomfortable than ever.

"I was wondering where you were headed?" she asked, hoping to get the conversation started.

"We are going west, Miss."

"I worked that out." Emer smiled but the girls didn't return her smile. They exchanged another look before one stared out the window. The second sent a glance at Emer before she started fiddling with the bag on her lap. Disappointed, Emer stood.

"Thank you for sharing your seat. I feel better now." She lied. The girl didn't hide the look of relief on her face. *Since when do my own class not speak to me?* As she walked, she passed a mirrored surface. An image of a wealthy young woman looked back at her. Only then did she smile slightly. *They thought you were rich. And they judged you, just as harshly as you judged Mrs.*

Shipley. Emer could hear Father Molloy's voice as clear as if he had been standing beside her. Head down, she walked back to the Shipley car, not bothering to acknowledge anyone she passed on her way.

"Back already, Miss Matthews. Did you have a nice walk?'

She nodded in response to Lawrence before taking a seat. Staring out the window, she did her best to ignore the man beside her. It didn't matter what his motive was. As soon as this trip was over, she would never see him again.

CHAPTER 17

"We will be in Denver tomorrow morning. The bank should be up and running by Monday morning at the latest. Your father said some man, Connors I think the name was, has strict instructions to have everything ready."

Lawrence ignored Mitchell. The Denver branch was his project, not his cousin's. He hid his annoyance over the fact Father had discussed the details. "When are you planning the grand opening, Mother?"

"A couple of days should be sufficient time to organize everything." His mother shifted her gaze to Emer. Before she could say anything, Lawrence jumped in.

"Are you coming to our grand opening, Miss Matthews?"

He smiled despite the look of horror on her face.

"Me? Sorry. I shall be on my way to Clover Springs."

"Of course you will, Miss Matthews. You are only staying with us for two nights. I promised Father Molloy I would look after you. I intend on keeping that promise."

Lawrence held his breath. Emer hadn't reacted favorably to previous commands from his mother. To his surprise, the young girl simply nodded and resumed looking out the window. Lawrence studied her. The black circles under her eyes were more pronounced than yesterday. Sleeping on a train was uncomfortable but he couldn't help feeling there was more to it than that.

"Mitchell, have you those plans Roland gave you? I wouldn't mind reading for a little bit."

"Plans? What plans? Mother, I warned you before. Denver is my project. Not yours and definitely not his." Lawrence sent a glare in the direction of his cousin.

"Lawrence, the bank is my business. All of the branches belong to your father." His mother's steel-laced tone was matched by the expression in her eyes.

"Mother, we have been through this before. I am taking over the Denver branch. I will make all of the decisions relevant to local business. I appreciate your offer of help but it is not necessary. Once you have organized your little soiree, I expect you to go back to Boston. Take him with you."

"Lawrence Shipley. How dare you speak to me like that, especially in front of… her."

"I am sure Miss Matthews finds this whole conversation as tedious as I do. In fact, now is a perfect time for lunch. Please excuse us, Mother. Miss Matthews and I will go to the dining car. We will see you later."

Lawrence sent a plea for understanding to Emer. He was delighted, although surprised, when she stood. "A snack sounds lovely. I'm starving."

Lawrence almost laughed out loud at his mother's expression. Ladies didn't comment on the fact that they were hungry. Nor did they agree to go to a meal unaccompanied. But Emer didn't care much for convention.

He followed her to the dining car, standing until she took her seat.

"Thank you for saving me."

Emer's eyes danced with merriment. "I didn't do it for you. I did it to upset your mother and her lapdog."

Lawrence nearly spurted the sip of water he had just taken on the table. Lapdog. It hadn't taken her long to see Mitchell for what he was. *What does she think of me?*

"I apologize to you, too, Miss Matthews."

"My name is Emer. Why are you saying you are sorry? You didn't do anything."

"I thought I may have upset you by asking questions about your family. I wasn't being nosey." At her upraised eyebrows, he held his hands up. "Well, maybe a little. I find you intriguing. You aren't like any other lady I ever met."

"I'm not a lady. I'm just a normal girl like many others. You don't see the likes of me as we don't usually dine in these places or wear these outfits."

"What would you usually wear?" Lawrence said idly, as the waiter put their plates on the table.

"Pants and a shirt." The waiter stopped serving them to stare at Emer. At a glance from Lawrence, he coughed, put the rest of the meal on the table and quickly moved away.

"I think your mother would have a stroke if she saw me."

"Will you tell me a little about yourself, Emer?" Lawrence asked, hoping he wouldn't frighten her away.

"There is nothing to tell. I left home when I was fifteen. I lived in a mining town for a couple of years before moving to Denver. I went to Boston to find my sister. I met Father Molloy, he introduced me to your family and we will arrive in Denver tomorrow. I will catch a train to Clover Springs and you will go play at being a banker."

Lawrence sat straighter. Emer was looking at him as if waiting to see his reaction to her insult.

"What will you do in Clover Springs?" He caught the glint of amusement in her eyes at his refusal to react.

"I will find my sister. After that, I don't know what I will do. I haven't really given it much thought."

"Well, we both know that's a lie. You cannot look at me and your face is turning a delightful shade of pink."

Emer moved to stand.

"Please, don't leave. I was only teasing. I'm bored. If I go back to that room, I may just kill my mother. You, Miss Matthews, have to save me from the hangman's rope."

Emer giggled.

"Why do you let your mother order you around like you're a child?"

"I don't." Lawrence looked at her, she returned his gaze but stayed silent. "I guess I do, don't I? Life is easier if I go along with her."

"Do you always pick the easy option?"

"Touché, Miss Matthews. I guess you got me back for teasing you earlier. I would love to tell my Mother to get lost, but…"

"Then you couldn't start your own bank. You think you need your family connections?"

"And you would suggest I don't?"

"I don't know the first thing about banking, Mr. Shipley. A friend of mine got rich lending small amounts of money to miners. She didn't have any family money behind her. But she's happy. Are you?"

Happy? He was. Wasn't he?

"Tell me more about your friend."

"Minnie bought a store up in Leadville. She learned early on the miners would miss home comforts."

Lawrence noticed the pause as well as the flush on her cheeks but pretended not to. She continued.

"She sold all manner of goods, from home ware through to tools and utensils they would need up in the mines. If a miner needed credit, she gave it to them in exchange for a grubstake in his mine."

"She trusted them to come back and tell her they had hit gold?" He couldn't hide the disbelief from his tone.

"She's a good judge of character. Well, most of the time, at least." Emer wasn't about to tell Lawrence about Minnie's whole story. "She told me once that only one miner ever held out on her."

"She sounds like a special lady. Is she still in Leadville?"

Emer shook her head before taking a sip of coffee. "She left to go overseas. She had a hankering to see London and some of Europe." Emer fiddled with her cup for a couple of seconds. "You could do something like Minnie did."

"Me? Grubstake miners? I don't think Mother would approve of that."

"I thought you wanted to get away from your mother. If you wanted to set up a new business out here, you could. You must have some money of your own." At her look, he nodded but didn't say anything.

"There are a lot of honest folk out west. They can't go into a bank. Some of them have never been near a big city. People like your mother wouldn't lend them a cent. So they fall victim to sharks. The men who make their money from other people's sweat and tears." Emer stopped talking.

He was staring at her and the look in his eyes made her uncomfortable. She fidgeted in her seat. "Sorry. Minnie told me I go on too much at times. I just hate people being taken advantage of."

"Actually, Miss Matthews, I think you may just have given me an idea. You are more than a pretty face, aren't you?"

He'd called her pretty. Warmth radiated through her whole body. She smiled.

"Especially when you smile like that."

She stood up quickly, embarrassed he had seen her reaction. "Thank you for the company. I am going to lie down for a while. You are right about it being difficult to sleep on a train."

Especially when every time you close your eyes, a pair of green eyes dominates your thoughts. Emer turned to leave, catching her foot in her skirt as she did. She stumbled and his hand flew out to steady her. His touch burned her skin. She glanced up at him to see his eyes widen. *He feels something, too. He must. There is no future in this. I have to get away. Now.* Picking up her skirt, she moved as quickly as possible without giving in to the impulse to run.

CHAPTER 18

DENVER

Denver was busier than she remembered. She wished Minnie was in town. At least then she would have one friend.

She wondered if Lewis was still around—not that she had any intention of looking him up. *Although it might be fun to introduce him to Mrs. Shipley.*

The streets teemed with people rushing about as if their boots were on fire. She'd decided to do some exploring to kill time. The trains for Clover Springs didn't run every day. She wasn't going to spend a minute more in the hotel where she was staying as a guest of Mrs. Shipley. It had been days since she could travel freely without Mrs. Shipley, Mitchell or Lawrence watching her, waiting for her to slip up. Again.

She wandered through a couple of streets before stopping at a café. Her stomach growled and the temptation to eat in peace, without anyone commenting on her manners or lack of them, proved too much. She ignored the disdainful looks from other customers. She didn't care if it was unseemly to eat alone. She was hungry and it wasn't as if she knew anyone else. Taking a seat by the window, she watched the crowds pass by as she ate her lunch. She ignored a couple of men who stared at her, hoping they wouldn't come closer. Wearing pants and carrying a gun, she was confident of her ability to defend herself but the dress and absence of a weapon made her feel naked.

She turned her attention back to the window just in time to see a child dart out onto the street. Horrified but frozen, she could only watch as a wagon moved toward the child. She screamed out to get the driver's attention but he couldn't hear her above the street noise. Rushing out of the café, she ran toward the child, not realizing the proprietor of the café had followed her, shouting, "Thief." Emer elbowed her way through the onlookers, having seen nobody was making any attempt to help the child.

"Another ragamuffin. A thief." Someone commented.

"What do you expect? The governor has his mind on the ladies, not on clearing the streets of rubbish like this." The crowd laughed at the man's remarks.

Fuming at the comments, Emer elbowed the men out of her way. Bending down, she reached for the child's hand. He was only about six or seven years old, the tears from his eyes marking two white paths down his dirty face. She forced herself to look at his legs. As she'd thought, one was pinned by the wagon. The boy's little body shook.

"Try to lie still. Don't move your legs." Silly as it sounded, it was important he didn't try to pull himself free. He could do more damage that way. Struggling to remember everything Pa Newmark had told her, Emer looked around her.

"You and you, we need to move the wagon. Gently, though."

Though surprised, the men acted without questioning her. Emer didn't have time to wonder why.

"Get a doctor, fast," she said to another child who was staring at the scene in front of him. He didn't move but stared back at her. "Go on. I'll pay you when you get back." The child took off, racing down the street.

Emer held the child as the men moved toward the wagon. "Can you help me drag him free?" she asked a man standing beside her.

"Sure thing, lady. You get out of my way, though. A little bitty thing like you ain't going to be able to drag anyone anywhere."

The man pushed Emer gently out of his way. Why

were people being so nice? *Because you are dressed like a wealthy young lady.*

Emer dismissed the thought. Focus on the child. The injured boy lost consciousness as the wagon moved, freeing his leg. As promised, the man dragged him clear. Without hesitating, Emer lifted her skirt and tore a piece of white fabric from her petticoat, for the first time thanking Mrs. Shipley for insisting she dress the part. A murmur arose from the crowd with several ladies turning their backs. *Oops, a real lady wouldn't show her ankles in public.*

Emer didn't care. All she was concerned about was the child. She had to stop the blood loss or he would be dead before the doctor arrived. Where was he, anyway?

Moving quickly but calmly, Emer secured a tourniquet around the boy's leg. She could hear Pa Newmark's voice in her head as she made sure it was secured tightly. Removing her jacket, she wrapped it around the child, shifting him gently onto her lap. She had to keep him as warm as possible. The man who had dragged him clear got some water.

"You some sort of nurse?"

Emer didn't get a chance to reply as they heard the doctor pushing his way through the crowd.

"Where's the lady who got hurt by the wagon? Excuse me, please. Let me through."

Emer glanced once more at her patient before turning her full attention to the doctor, who seemed to have been struck dumb.

"Where are you hurt?" he asked Emer, looking confused at the child on her lap.

"I am not hurt. This child got hit by a wagon. His leg is bleeding real bad. I tied it up but that isn't going to last long. He needs proper medical attention."

"You mean to say, you called *me* to give attention to a street rat!"

Emer's temper rose. "I called for a doctor to help a child."

Her protest went unnoticed by the physician who had already turned his back, apparently with the intention of leaving.

"Miss, you owe me. I got the doctor."

Emer glared at the child badgering her for money and he took a step back from the fire in her eyes. "Doctor, where are you going? You have a patient to see to."

"I only see paying patients. Good day to you."

"Send the bill to Mrs. Shipley." Emer crossed her fingers, hoping the ruse would work.

The crowd surged forward, waiting to hear the doctor's response. "Shipley. You are related to the Shipley family?"

The doctor didn't bother to hide his disbelief.

"No, she isn't, but I am. I'm Lawrence Shipley. What is the problem?"

"This doctor," Emer's tone bristled with contempt, "refuses to attend to this child. He seems to believe only the rich are worthy of medical attention." The sarcasm dripping from Emer's words had the desired effect on the crowd. The murmuring grew louder in its condemnation of the doctor, who paled as he seemed to realize the precarious nature of his position.

"The…girl is mistaken. What I meant was, I cannot examine the child in the middle of the street. Danger of infection."

"The *lady* has already started treating your patient while you have yet to look at him. I suggest you remedy that quickly."

Emer watched Lawrence's face. He didn't follow through on the implied threat. He didn't have to. The doctor jumped to do his bidding. He moved to examine the child. "He'll have to go to the hospital. The leg has to come off."

Emer cuddled the boy closer to her as the crowd parted to make way for a wagon. She didn't see Lawrence until he had bent down beside her. "Let me." He gently took the injured child from her arms.

"Lawrence, we have to go with him. I don't trust that doctor. Not one little bit."

Lawrence looked at her for a few minutes. "My

carriage is over there. We will take the child to the hospital. Travers, pay this quack, will you." More than one person in the crowd smiled at the reaction of the doctor to the insult delivered by the gentleman.

"Miss Matthews. Emer? Are you coming?"

Emer focused at Lawrence's tone. Standing up, she brushed down her dress, noting the blood stains. How was she going to explain all this to Mrs. Shipley?

"Excuse me, Miss, but you said you'd pay me to get the doctor." The boy she had dispatched earlier stood looking at her, his hunger evident not just in his pale, drawn face but his too-thin body. "I'm sorry I got a wrong 'un." He looked so downcast, she couldn't bear it. She fished inside her reticule and handed him some change. The boy's face lit up. "Thank you, Miss. Ma will be so happy."

The boy ran off as Emer climbed into the back of the carriage. She put the young boy's head on her lap after glancing at the bandage she had applied. There was no sign of fresh bleeding. Was that a good or a bad sign?

It didn't take long to reach Denver General. Lawrence took the child and carried him inside. His manner commanded attention and soon the best doctors in the city were treating the little boy. Emer sat on a hard chair until the doctors finished their assessment. She was glad Lawrence had disappeared. She couldn't deal with him at the moment.

Some time later, she spotted Lawrence with another man. They walked toward her. She stood, trying to get her tongue unstuck from the roof of her mouth. She needed some water. But there was no time for that.

The man with Lawrence started talking. She listened as he explained about the boy. Luckily, the damage hadn't been as bad as they'd first thought. The child wouldn't lose his leg. The bone, although broken, was a clean break. With luck, it would set properly. After a couple of days' stay in hospital, the child should return to full health. Assuming, of course, no infection set in.

"Are you the young lady who nursed the child?"

Emer looked at the kindly-faced man standing in front of her. Before she could answer, Lawrence introduced her.

"Miss Matthews, this is Dr. Watkins. Dr. Brown, the man we met on the street, is his boss."

Emer caught the irritated look in the doctor's eyes at the mention of his colleague but then it was gone.

"Miss Matthews. Excuse me for saying this, but you look very young to be a nurse."

"I'm not a nurse, Sir."

"Yet, you knew exactly what to do. Your attentiveness saved that boy's leg, if not his life."

"I had a friend. He was a doctor in the war. He taught me some things."

"He must be very proud of his student. If you decide on becoming a nurse, please call back to see me. We could always do with skills like yours here at Denver General." The doctor walked away, leaving Emer staring after him.

"You can close your mouth now, Miss Matthews."

Emer glanced at Lawrence. "He asked me if I was a nurse. Nobody ever asked me anything like that before."

"You are a lady with many hidden talents."

His praise brought her skin out in goose bumps. She looked away for fear he would see the effect he had on her.

"Now, my dear, do you think we could go home? Mother has guests this evening. She will not take kindly to us appearing in this state."

She took his arm and allowed him to escort her out of the hospital. He helped her into the cab, holding her for a few seconds longer than seemed necessary. His smell reminded her of early days spent lying in the grass enjoying the sunshine. Happy days when she had been too innocent to understand what her ma did. Ma. Why did Patty have to intrude on her thoughts now? *Lawrence wouldn't give you a second look if he knew about her.*

Lawrence had been right. His mother nearly had an apoplectic fit when she saw the state of Emer's dress. Lawrence took pleasure in filling her in on the details, including how she had used her petticoat to make a bandage. Mrs. Shipley had turned various shades of red before banishing Emer to her room for the evening. Emer could have sworn from Lawrence's wink this was exactly his intention.

CHAPTER 19

Lawrence didn’t look at Emer as she left the room. He didn’t want his mother seeing how much their guest intrigued him. Emer was totally different than any other girl he had met. She had captured his attention on the train but he had put it down to being an interesting distraction on an otherwise boring trip. But it was more than that. Much more. She was feisty and kind-hearted but her manners were appalling.

She wouldn't be an asset to a banker as she couldn't be trusted not to scandalize the wealthy clients the business depended on. Life wouldn't be as dull as ditchwater with her around.

He poked the fire, wondering why he was so on edge. He had fought hard to get to manage the Denver office but now that he was here, the challenge had gone. Was that what Emer was? A fresh target for him to conquer. All his life he had played second fiddle to his father first and then his older brother. He wanted to show his father he was the right man for this job, but was the job the right match for him?

"Lawrence, do you have to spend time with that girl? It is going to reflect badly on you, not to mention the whole family."

"Why, Mother? I thought your ladies would be impressed by our act of charity."

"Our customers are impressed when we hand over cold hard cash. They do not expect us to mingle with ruffians. Imagine the scandal if our friends were to find out that... that girl showed off her body in public."

"Only her ankles, Mother, and very pretty ones at that."

His mother's nostrils flared as she turned the full force of her anger in his direction.

"Stop behaving like a boor, Lawrence. Our reputation means everything. You have seen what Denver is doing to Mr. Talbot. The poor man."

"I'm surprised, Mother. I thought you would take Mrs. Talbot's side, the first Mrs. Talbot, that is. Public sympathy is very much behind her."

Lawrence concealed a grin as his mother digested this piece of news. He would bet his last dollar his precious mother would be calling on Augusta Talbot very soon. That was the thing about his parents. You knew exactly what they were going to do next. They would do anything to increase the bank profits or the family reputation, preferably both. He couldn't resist teasing his mother.

"Aren't you going to ask how the young boy is?"

"What young boy?" Mrs. Shipley looked at Lawrence closely. "Are you jesting with me, Lawrence?"

"Would I?" Before she could answer, he stood to kiss her cheek. "Goodnight, Mother. I have a date with some cards and a fine cigar."

CHAPTER 20

Lawrence didn't take the buggy. Instead, he walked. He wanted to call into Denver General to check on the boy. He admired Doctor Watkins but he wouldn't put it past Doctor Brown to throw the boy out on the street. He was determined the child would get the best of care. *Emer would be happy. That's not the only reason, is it?*

Arriving at the hospital, he was pleasantly surprised to find the boy awake. He didn't seem too bad considering the ordeal he'd been through. His parents were by his bedside. They seemed uncomfortable in his presence. The father tipped his cap to Lawrence before his wife pushed him forward. "The wife and me, we'd like to thank ya for your kindness. Our boy is all we have left." The man looked away but not before Lawrence saw his eyes glistening with emotion.

"Your son will be fine. He is to stay in the hospital for a few days but he will get the best of care"

"Thank ya kindly, Sir. But, well, the wife and me don't have money for the hospital bills. Doctor Watkins, he was kind and said we could stay but then Doctor Brown said we must move him immediately."

A red mist descended. "We'll see about that." Lawrence's tone caused the couple to shrink back from him. The child didn't move but stared up at him, his face as pale as the sheets on the bed. "Please do not leave. I will be back."

Lawrence marched through the ward until he spotted a nurse. "Nurse, get me whomever is in charge of this hospital."

"But Sir, its late."

"I said now." The nurse scurried away, he assumed to do his biding. He paced back and forth, his temper rising with every second he waited. How dare Brown contradict his express orders!

Finally, a rather disheveled man appeared back with the nurse.

"You asked to see me, Sir?" The man's irony was not lost on Lawrence. Neither was the stern look on his face. "I have left a patient. This better be important and not the actions of some youngster who likes to throw his father's money around."

Lawrence would have smiled but for his temper.

He stared at the older man but it had no effect. He simply stared back.

"Today, I told one of your doctors to treat a patient. Tonight, I find he has disobeyed me and told the parents to remove the patient from this hospital."

"Are you a physician?"

Lawrence shook his head.

"Then by what right do you have to tell my doctors how to behave? Their professional opinion is all that matters. Good evening. I have patients to attend to."

"Wait. If he was a professional, I would have no argument. But this ...doctor initially refused to treat the patient, despite him being in danger of bleeding to death on a street corner."

"Mister..." The man waited

"Shipley of Shipley Bank"

"I am aware of your family, Sir. I can assure you our doctors do not behave in the manner you have outlined. There must be a mistake."

"Brown is the man's name. He deemed the child unworthy of treatment as there was some question over his ability to meet the bill."

The physician had the grace to look embarrassed. "That is unfortunate. Our hospital must prioritize those that can pay their debts. I must back Doctor Brown on his decision.

"I will meet all costs. The child will remain here until he is fit enough to return home. While here, he is to have the best of everything, including the medical staff caring for him. Do I make myself clear?"

"Yes, Sir."

"For the record, if you claim to know my family, you will also know my parents make regular donations to the upkeep of this hospital. They wouldn't like to hear about what happened this evening."

"Of course not, Sir."

Lawrence marched back down the corridor to where he had left the boy's parents. He didn't like bullying anyone but sometimes having money, power and position came in useful!

* * *

THE NEXT DAY, Emer returned to the café. "I am so sorry I forgot to pay my bill yesterday."

"It has already been settled, Miss. Your gentleman friend paid it last evening. Left a generous tip, too." The café owner's smile grew wider. "Would you like to see today's menu?"

"No, thank you. I have another appointment." Emer walked quickly out of the café before the owner persuaded her to sit and eat. Lawrence had come to her rescue. *Again.*

She went back to the hospital to visit the young boy. Doctor Brown, or the quack as Lawrence had called him, was nowhere to be seen. Relieved to find the child awake, Emer took a seat by the bed. Some time later, the boy's parents came in to visit him. "Ma, Pa, this is the lady who saved me yesterday."

"I didn't do anything." Embarrassed, Emer rose to her feet. Before she could do anything, she was drawn into a hug by the boy's mother. "We lost our other babies on the way here. We only stopped in Denver so Craig, my husband, could make some money. Thank you for saving our boy."

Seeing the love this small family had for one another, Emer couldn't help but wish her background had been similar. She sniffed, trying but failing to stop the tears leaking from her eyes. Unable to say anything, she returned the woman's hug and shook the man's hand.

"Please say thank you to Mr. Shipley. If he hadn't paid the doctor, we wouldn't be here."

Stunned, Emer stared at the mother. *Lawrence had come to see the boy*. He was totally different from his mother.

Emer took her leave of the small family and headed back to the Shipley mansion. She couldn't wait to thank Lawrence in person.

CHAPTER 21

"Miss Matthews, will you please at least try to behave like a lady"

Lawrence hesitated as he put his hand on the doorknob. The door was open but he didn't enter. He knew that tone. His mother was beyond angry. He grimaced as she continued.

"I know you're an orphan. I have tried to be patient. Goodness knows how hard I've tried. I have a reputation to consider. Not just mine, but that of Shipley bank."

Lawrence had heard enough. He was about to enter the room when he heard Emer answer, her tone matching his mothers.

"Mrs. Shipley, I am not an orphan. I have a ma. Thank you for taking me to Denver. I am leaving now."

Lawrence wanted to applaud the young girl who was taking on his mother. Lord knows she deserved it after the way she had behaved over the years. He pushed the door open, eager to witness the confrontation in person.

* * *

"WHY, OF ALL THE UNGRATEFUL..."

Emer saw the door open and watched as Lawrence slipped into the room. His mother was too wound up to notice. She couldn't stay here, not with him watching. She wasn't some sideshow in a circus set up for his amusement. *Or maybe that was exactly how he saw her.*

Shaking, she stood up so quickly the chair she had been sitting on fell backwards. Emer didn't even look at it. Instead, she glared at the woman who had made her life miserable over the last few days. "Listen, lady, you only helped me because it made you look good in front of Father Molloy. I am not some cause. I don't need charity."

Remembering at the last second she wasn't wearing pants, Emer picked up her skirts and ran. She kept running until she reached the garden. She had to get away from Mrs. Shipley or she may do the woman an injury. She wasn't an orphan, although it might have been better if she was. She stopped running, trying to get her breath back.

Walking more slowly, she made her way over to the swing she had spotted earlier. It was a lovely day, despite being a bit chilly. She sat on the swing, moving backward and forward slightly. What was she going to do now? Did she have enough money to get to Clover Springs? What would she do when she got there? Maybe she could go back to Denver General, find kind Dr. Watkins and work as a nurse for a while until she had the money to travel on. No, she had to get out of Denver. Lawrence was here and she couldn't risk bumping into him. *He had no place in her world.*

LAWRENCE WORKED HARD KEEPING a straight face as his mother ranted over the events of the afternoon. Finally, she'd worked herself into such a state, he insisted she lie down.

Emer. Where was she now? The servants said she had run toward the garden but that had been some time ago. Taking his jacket, he set out to find her.

Walking through the gardens, he heard the unmistakable sounds of sobbing. He stopped, wondering whether he should leave her alone. She wouldn't thank him for seeing her crying, but then, he was too much of a gentleman to ignore a lady in distress.

He moved toward her, deliberately walking heavily

to alert her to his presence. It didn't work. She was so caught up in her heartbreak, she didn't seem aware of him.

The late sun glinted off her hair, making the blonde streaks look whiter. Her lush lips looked brighter against the pallor of her skin. How he longed to crush her against him and kiss her. *She'd probably hit me.*

"Lawrence, what are you doing here?" she sniffed before wiping her nose on her sleeve. He grinned, thinking of his mother's reaction to such unladylike behavior. Handing her his hanky, he said softly, "I think you won the argument. My mother has taken to her bed."

Emer sniffed.

"Emer, you really shouldn't listen to her. She has some old fashioned ideas about how things should work. It's hard to believe she wasn't born wearing a bustle."

Emer smiled at the clothing reference but unlike so many girls of her age, she didn't blush or admonish him for rudeness.

"My darling mother was the daughter of a miner." That got her attention. "She may look and act like a lady but Grandpa Joe wasn't a gentleman. He headed to California back in the 1840s. He was lucky. He found some gold but quickly realized the real way to make money was to sell stuff to other miners. He used his gold to set up his first store and then another and another. Minnie, the lady you mentioned on the train, reminded me of him."

He saw her eyes widen at the fact he remembered her friend's name.

"Grandpa married well. My grandmother was a lady but her family was impoverished." At her confused look, he explained. "Dirt poor due to her father's gambling problem."

Emer drew in a sharp breath.

"Don't look so shocked. Most of the wealthy families in Boston and other areas made their money in similar ways. Mother likes to believe different and she makes everyone else pretend, too. But the reality is, she is the daughter of a miner turned storekeeper. Grandpa Joe, he was a real character." He stopped talking to swallow the lump of loss he got when thinking of his Grandpa. The man died shortly after Lawrence completed his two years at the bank. Lawrence clenched his hands at the thought of what his parents had stolen from him. Contrary to what his father had said, Grandpa Joe hadn't agreed with his parents' decision to make him pursue a career in banking. He had wanted Lawrence to join him but didn't want to come between his daughter and grandson. How he wished he had. He would give anything to have more time with his Grandpa.

"You would have liked him, I think. Anyway, he

loved his wife, Lily, and to please her he sent his girls East to be educated. Mother and her sisters attended finishing school where they learned how to land rich husbands. She met my father and the rest, as they say, is history."

"Your mother seems so—well, so ..."

"Dignified and ladylike. Grandpa Joe would tell you his money was well spent. Mother didn't like us visiting him as children as he would tell us stories of the old days. Can't imagine my mother climbing a tree or using an outhouse, can you?"

Lawrence deliberately tried to be shocking in the hope of making Emer laugh. He smiled as she giggled.

"I think part of the reason she is being so horrid to you is you remind her of herself."

The smile disappeared. "I am nothing like your mother."

He took her hands in his. "No, you're not. You have a kind heart underneath that tough exterior."

He stroked her hands, wanting to pull her toward him. *He wanted... what did he want?*

Emer pulled her hands free. "Now you're teasing me."

He stepped toward her, putting his hand under her chin, he forced her to look up and meet his gaze.

"Not now."

Before she could react, he leaned in and brushed his lips against hers. She murmured but didn't push him away. He kissed her eyes, the tip of her nose before claiming one more kiss on her lips. Pulling her closer to him, he held his head against hers. "You intrigue me, Miss Matthews. Emer."

He kissed the top of her hair before they heard someone coming. Springing apart, he put a finger to his lips urging her to stay silent. He didn't want to risk the servants finding them like this. It would do nothing for her reputation.

Stunned by his kisses, Emer couldn't move. Her legs felt weak and her heart was hammering so hard, it felt like it would explode from her chest. She had been embraced before but it had never been like that. Her whole body had reacted to him, making her yearn for something she didn't understand. But she understood one thing. Lawrence Shipley wasn't the man for her. He came from a different world, one in which there was no home for her. She had to get away from him before her feelings overwhelmed her completely.

Now she understood why Minnie had stood by Lewis all that time and would take him back in a heartbeat. If she could feel this strongly after such a short period of time, what would she feel in a year? It was time to leave—although she had a sinking feeling it was already too late.

CHAPTER 22

"Miss Matthews, before you leave this afternoon, would you care to visit the bank with me?"

"Lawrence, I am sure Miss Matthews has better things to do with her time." Mrs. Shipley glared at her son over the breakfast table. Emer hadn't been able to leave the previous day, having found out the train left today at noon.

"Actually, I'd love to. I haven't been in a bank before. Do I get to see where the gold is kept? Perhaps you could show me, Lawrence."

Lawrence laughed as Emer fluttered her eyelashes in an obvious attempt to upset his mother. *Show her the gold, indeed.* She was play-acting the part of a gold digger to perfection for his mother's benefit. It was working, too. His mother looked fit to spit.

"Shall we leave now?" Lawrence wiped his hands with the gleaming white napkin before standing.

"I'm coming, too."

Lawrence almost groaned aloud at his cousin's announcement. He hadn't liked him much in Boston but after being confined in close quarters with him on the train, he disliked him intensely.

"There is no need, Mitchell. It won't take two of us."

"There is every need, Lawrence." His mother's tone brooked no argument. He shrugged his shoulders, not meeting Emer's eyes. He was certain from her slightly shaking arms she was laughing.

The trip to the bank was conducted in silence. Lawrence hid behind a paper while Emer looked out the window.

Mitchell made an attempt at conversation but, when they both ignored him, he gave up. Lawrence sent a conspiratorial wink at Emer, who grinned back before staring back out the window. It didn't take long to reach the bank.

"You go ahead, Mitchell. I will assist Miss Matthews."

Mitchell didn't argue. Lawrence held his hand up to Emer who was looking around her, a small smile of satisfaction on her face.

"Does it meet with your approval, Miss Matthews?"

"Why, yes, kind Sir. When I have accumulated my savings, I will surely visit this here establishment." Emer didn't continue as they were both laughing so hard. "Sorry, Lawrence. I shouldn't tease you so much."

Yes, you should. You make me laugh. You make every day an adventure. Life without you is going to be so boring. Instead of speaking his mind, Lawrence simply held her hand. He was in no position to declare anything to Miss Matthews. What did he want, anyway? She wasn't a saloon girl. Despite his mother's opinion, she was respectable. But was she marriage material? *Marriage? Since when had he started thinking about getting married.*

He introduced Emer to various members of the staff. She was kind and polite, asking each person something about themselves. For her youth, she had a way of putting people at ease. There was something about her. Her infectious smile perhaps, or the humor in her eyes.

"Everything on target, Connors?"

"Yes, Mr. Shipley," the head cashier answered. "Perhaps we could have coffee in your office. I took the liberty of setting three places."

"That was kind of you, Collins," Mitchell said as he took a seat.

"It's Connors, Sir, not Collins."

Connors' tone was respectful but distant. *Not a bit*

like the man himself. Lawrence wondered what had gone on between the two men. Connors got on with everyone. It was part of why he was so successful.

"Thank you, Connors. I am sure Mitchell can find a cup of coffee elsewhere. Close the door behind you, Mitchell. There's a good man." Lawrence turned to Emer. "Would you like to pour, Miss Matthews? Connors likes his with cream."

Emer grinned and rose to pour. Connors sat but didn't say a word until Mitchell banged the door behind him.

"Sorry, Sir, but there is just something not right. I don't mean any disrespect but he asks so many questions. He's worse than…" Connors's cheeks burned bright.

"My mother. Yes, he is. Let's enjoy our coffee and then while Miss Matthews takes a tour, we can have a quick talk. Will that work?"

Emer took the hint and finished her coffee quickly. She made her excuses and left the two bankers to their discussions.

Wandering around the beautiful building, she could see Mrs. Shipley's eye for detail. There wasn't a speck of dust on any of the furnishings. The whole place looked impressive but forbidding. She couldn't imagine any of the miners bringing their gold into a place like this. But then the Shipleys weren't interested in people like that. *People like me.*

Lawrence was frowning when he came out of his meeting with Connors. It seemed to Emer as if he couldn't get out of the bank fast enough.

"Miss Matthews, we best hurry if you are going to get your train."

They caught a cab to the train station. "Mr. Connors seems like a nice man," Emer said but Lawrence didn't respond. He was distracted. *Can't wait to get rid of me, I guess.*

He walked her to the train car, holding the car door open for her with one hand, her bag in the other. He steered her toward a private car. "I thought you might prefer the privacy. I sent a telegram to Clover Springs advising your sister of your arrival."

"Thank you, Lawrence. Your family has already been so kind."

"No, we haven't. Mother hasn't a kind bone in her body. You, on the other hand, well..."

She waited, not daring to breathe as he stammered. Was he nervous? Or was it something else?

"Oh, heck, Emer, couldn't you stay in Denver a while longer? We could see if— well, maybe there would be a way..."

"Thank you, Lawrence, but you best get off the train or you will be traveling, too." Emer tried her best to make a joke. She didn't want him to see how upset she was. She busied herself taking off her coat. She took her bag and their fingers touched. The electricity between them sparked once more. With an oath, he took her into his arms and kissed her soundly. Then he was gone.

CHAPTER 23

The smoke from the train blurred her vision as she arrived in Clover Springs. She dusted off the worst of the dust from her traveling costume. She would have worn pants and a shirt but her experiences with the Shipleys dictated she should at least try to conform. She wanted to make a good impression on Sorcha, her big sister.

She stood, then sat down and stood up again. She couldn't sit still. What if her sister hated her? What if she didn't want any reminders of their mother? What if she hated Sorcha? Was she like Patty? *Of course she isn't like Ma. She never knew her.*

"Clover Springs." The conductor's voice announcing they had arrived at the town broke into her frenzied thoughts. It was too late to have doubts now.

Emer stood, rubbing her hands down the folds of her skirt. Looking around to make sure she hadn't forgotten anything, she walked slowly toward the door of the car. Thank God the Shipleys had stayed in Denver. If she had to spend one second longer with Mrs. Shipley, she'd have been in no fit state to meet her sister. Mrs. Raines was right. She was a cold, old witch.

Emer stepped out onto the platform and immediately heard her name. A girl who looked too much like her not to be Sorcha came running toward her, her skirts held up in one hand.

All too soon, she was enveloped in a hug. Her sister's face was wet with tears. The hug lasted a few seconds before Sorcha pushed her away.

"Let me look at you. I can't believe you are here. My baby sister."

Sorcha's sincere welcome and her kind tone was a balm to Emer after all she had endured at the hands of Mrs. Shipley.

"Hello, Sorcha."

Sorcha hugged her close once more. Emer tried to be as affectionate in return but it was difficult. Cuddles and affection hadn't played a huge part in her childhood and her movements were awkward. She saw a hint of hurt in her sister's eyes. She pulled the older girl closer trying to dispel it.

"I'm sorry. I stink. The trip took longer than I

thought. I couldn't stay in Denver a second longer. I had to get away."

"From who? Did someone hurt you? Tell me who it was. Nobody is allowed to hurt my family."

Family. She was part of a real family.

"It's over now." Emer averted her gaze. *It was all over. She'd never see Lawrence again.*

"Ma, are you going to let us meet our aunt?"

Emer looked over Sorcha's shoulder to find two girls looking back at her. Sorcha pulled out of the embrace but didn't let go of Emer. "These are my girls. Jenny and Meggie, say hello to your Aunt Emer."

The girls came forward and joined the hug. Meggie lifted her arms up. When Emer didn't react, Sorcha bent down and picked up the little girl. "Meggie, Emer is a bit shy. You have to let her get to know you, all right?" Sorcha turned to Emer. "Come and meet my husband Brian."

Brian was so tall and broad, he made Sorcha look even smaller. The look he gave his wife made Emer's throat swell. It was easy to see the couple were happily married.

"Nice to meet you at last, Emer. Can I take your bags?" Brian hadn't hugged her but simply shaken her hand.

"Brian's sister, Nandita, is away visiting family at the moment. She will be back in a few days." Sorcha's eyes danced in her face. "Would you like to go for some lunch or come home and freshen up first?"

Emer was starving but having lunch meant meeting more people.

"I'd love to freshen up first, please."

"Ma baked cookies. They're good, too." Meggie lisped, giving Sorcha a big cuddle.

CHAPTER 24

The trip to the homestead didn't seem long as the girls asked Emer lots of questions about the trip. Sorcha needed reassurance Father Molloy wasn't too badly injured. Emer made them laugh with tales of how Mrs. Raines was killing the old man with kindness, making him rest and behave.

"It wouldn't surprise me if he turned up here one day, having run away from her."

Everyone laughed and the pain in Emer's stomach started to subside. She was touched when Sorcha prepared a bath for her, giving her time alone to bathe and wash her hair. Brian was working in the barn. Sorcha took the girls out to pick some apples. Time alone was exactly what she needed.

She looked around her at her sister's home. It wasn't big, especially in comparison to the Shipley mansion. But where the mansion had been cold and uninviting, this was comfortable and homey.

Sunlight shone through the gleaming windows, causing every surface to sparkle, not a speck of dust in sight. The main room smelled of honeysuckle and beeswax. The table had a lace centerpiece with a jar of wild flowers in its center.

In the kitchen, she spotted a black range, scrubbed to a shine. Even the wood was stacked neatly in the wood box.

Her sister was a good homemaker. This was a real home. For a second, she envied the children growing up in this house surrounded by the love of a mother and father.

Wonder if she learned homemaking at the orphanage or did our grandmother teach her? It certainly wasn't an inherited trait. Patty wouldn't know how to keep a house clean. She dismissed thoughts of Patty. She wasn't about to let her ma ruin this time with her sister.

Soon she heard giggling and the door opened, admitting the two girls closely followed by her sister.

"Did you get a chance to rest?"

"Thank you for the lovely bath. It was so nice to wash all that grime out of my hair."

"Your hair is pretty. It looks like Ma's." Meggie came toward Emer but she was a little hesitant. Emer saw the uncertainty on the child's face. She had to be the one to make the first move this time. Her unconscious rejection at the train station hadn't gone unnoticed.

Emer put out her arms and the child ran into them, giving her a big cuddle. Tears immediately filled her eyes. Embarrassed, she looked away until she got her feelings under control. When Sorcha spoke, her voice sounded wobbly.

"Meggie has a big heart. She has lots of love to go around. Enough for all of us."

Emer cuddled the child close before setting her back down. Spotting Jenny looking at her, she smiled at the older girl who seemed shy. "I am sure you are a great help to Sorcha. The house is so clean." Jenny beamed with pride.

Emer sat as instructed. She watched her sister as she worked, talking the whole time she moved around the kitchen. She shook the stove grates before adding more wood to the fire. Soon, an appetizing smell filled the room. Emer's stomach grumbled in response, causing Meggie to laugh.

They sat and ate together, letting the girls chatter away about their day. Brian didn't say a lot. Emer caught a couple of questioning glances sent her way but any time she met his eyes, he just smiled. Emer sensed Sorcha had lots of questions but she wanted to wait until they were alone. How would she answer them?

CHAPTER 25

The time flew past. Soon the girls were in bed. Emer helped Sorcha with the last of the chores, wondering how long Brian would be out in the barn. She wasn't sure she could deal with two people questioning her.

"Brian had to call over to the Sullivan ranch to check on one of their horses. It gives us time to talk." Sorcha pulled the rocking chairs closer to the fire. "I thought it might be easier if he wasn't here. I have so many questions and I guess you do, too."

"Were you happy?" Emer blurted out the question that had consumed her since she first learned her ma had considered leaving her at the orphanage.

Sorcha looked into the fire. Emer shifted in her seat, the pain on her sister's face making her uncomfortable. "You don't have to tell me."

"No, I do. I was happy with granny. She wasn't a sweet old lady like you read about in stories. She was loud and shouted a lot but she cared. She really tried to make life better for me. She let everyone believe she was my ma. Tried to protect me. I believed her, until the other kids told me different."

Emer yearned to touch her sister but seeing Sorcha's arms drawn across her chest, she didn't move.

"When Granny died, there was no one so they took me to the nuns. I hated it in that place. Some of the nuns were kind but the Reverend Mother—she was a real witch."

Emer shivered at the venom in Sorcha's voice.

"She didn't tell me about you until I was leaving. In fact, I think she never planned on telling me. She was angry and let it slip. I thought she was being mean. I didn't believe I had a sister. Granny would have told me." Sorcha brushed the tears from her face. She held out her hands to Emer. "You have no idea how much I wanted a family of my own. And now you are here."

"You have a family. The girls are lovely. You mentioned Brian had a sister and Brian seems…"

"Quiet! Yes, he is but I love him and the girls. Nandita is a good friend. You are my sister. I feel like I know you already and we just met."

Emer looked at the fire. She couldn't meet her sister's eyes. It would hurt her if she said she didn't feel the same, yet she couldn't lie. But would it be a lie?

Emer glanced at Sorcha and saw the disappointment on her face but it was quickly replaced by curiosity.

"What is Ma like? I mean, is she still alive? She didn't die, did she?"

"She was alive two years ago." Emer tried to keep her tone light.

"Do you know where she is? Do you think if I wrote her, she'd come and visit? Maybe if she knew you were here, she'd settle in Clover Springs and we could be a real family."

Emer laughed but the harsh sound was anything but happy.

"Patty isn't interested in family. Believe me, Sorcha, you are better off not knowing that woman. She's poison." Emer bit her lip as her sister went pale, tears glistening in her eyes. *Why had she said that? She didn't have to tell the truth.*

"You can't mean that. I know she's not perfect. Nobody who leaves their child and runs is. Maybe she's wiser now she's older. She didn't dump you at the orphanage."

"No, but she would have left me with her ma if the old woman was up for it." Emer ignored Sorcha's intake of breath. "Father Molloy told me Patty tried to persuade her ma to take me but Sadie said she was too old. I don't know why she didn't dump me at the orphanage. I wish she had."

"I wish she'd kept me. I would have done anything for a real ma." Sorcha put her head in her hands and cried. Emer stood but instead of comforting her sister, she started pacing the floor.

"Like you?"

Sorcha lifted her head. "What does that mean?"

"You're a real ma. You keep a nice house, you cook and clean. You even bake cookies. Our ma never did any of that. I don't think she knows how."

Sorcha stared at her wide eyed but Emer couldn't stop.

"You got to get rid of this idea that ma was some sort of saint. She wasn't. Even Father Molloy wouldn't be able to see any good in her, if he ever has the misfortune to meet her."

"Emer, stop it. She can't be that bad. She just can't."

"She is! Do yourself a favor and forget all about our ma. In fact, while you are at it, forget about this whole thing. I was wrong to come here."

Emer moved quickly to the door and would have run but for the fact Brian was standing there. The shock on his face hit home. She turned behind her to find Sorcha sitting on the chair, knees drawn up like a child, sobbing her heart out. She hadn't even noticed her sister's distress. She was too consumed with her own pain.

"Sorry, I've got to get some air." Emer brushed past

her sister's husband and headed outside. She had to walk or she would burst.

CHAPTER 26

Emer walked till she came to the creek Sorcha had pointed out earlier. The sound of the rippling water helped sooth her frazzled mood. Some time passed before she felt Sorcha standing behind her.

"I'm sorry. I had no right to upset you." Emer apologized.

"No, it's me who should say I am sorry. Brian warned me that your—I mean, our story wasn't going to be like one of the fairytales I tell the kids."

"He's a sensible man," Emer said, trying to distract Sorcha. She wasn't sure she was able to talk about Patty again. The need to tell her sister everything was too strong to fight. She couldn't, though. It would destroy her and Patty had ruined enough lives.

"Did Father Molloy not tell you anything?" Emer

wasn't sure how much of her story the priest had put in his letter.

"Not really. He said I should have patience. He tried to warn me not to push you to tell me everything at once. I didn't listen. I'm sorry." Sorcha's voice quivered with suppressed tears. Emer wanted to make her feel better but she didn't really know how.

"Ma isn't all bad," Emer found herself saying. "She has some redeeming qualities. She's good at telling stories, a bit like you, I guess."

The smile on Sorcha's face was worth the small lie. Ma was good at telling stories, all right. It was the truth she had issues with.

"Where does she live?"

"Kansas." At the look of hope on Sorcha's face, Emer continued quickly. "Well, that's where she was two years ago but she likes to move around. Restless spirit, I guess. She says it's the Irish in her." Emer forced a yawn.

At once, Sorcha was all apologies.

"Emer, I'm sorry. You are very tired. Come on back to the house and go to bed. We can talk about Ma tomorrow or the next day. There's no rush."

Emer let Sorcha take her arm as they both walked back to the house. Brian looked up from his book. Emer thought she saw a touch of understanding alongside the wariness in his eyes but she didn't know him well enough to be sure. He didn't say anything other than, "Goodnight."

Emer tossed and turned, the quiet of the house making her thoughts seem louder. *This was a huge mistake. I need to leave.*

There was no point in being careless. It was madness to go wandering the prairie in the darkness. She got up and dressed but waited until the first hint of daybreak. She didn't want to risk meeting Brian—or worse, her sister.

She left a note on her pillow.

"Dear Sorcha,

Thank you for welcoming me to your home. You have a lovely family. I wanted to see you were happy. Please don't try to stop me leaving. It is for the best.

Emer

CHAPTER 27

She remembered the route to town. The long walk would give her time to shed her tears and get her emotions under control. Her sister was happy and she didn't want to ruin that. It was best she leave. As the sun moved higher in the sky, she was glad of the shelter from the cottonwoods.

By the time she arrived in town, she was tired and thirsty. She looked around for a café but could only see a general store. She walked toward it, confident the owner would give her directions to a café. Pushing open the door, she was delighted to find a young woman behind the till. The storekeeper was talking to a young child. Before she got to speak to her, another woman came in the door behind her. Her pregnant form filled the doorway.

"Morning, Sorcha. No, you're not Sorcha? Sorry,

the sun was in my eyes. Oh, my. You're Emer, aren't you?"

"Mary, take a seat before you fall over and leave our visitor alone." The storekeeper turned to Emer. "Please excuse my friend and sister- in- law. She could chat for Ireland."

"Mary and Katie. Father Molloy's girls," Emer said looking from one to the other. "He described you both to me."

"I so wish he could have come with you. Did you bring Sorcha with you?" Mary asked as she took the seat Katie brought out to her.

Emer looked around the store as she tried to keep her voice steady. "Sorcha had chores so I thought I would take a walk into town."

"Hmm. Did you think the Petersens would steal your stuff?"

Emer tugged at her skirts, trying to hide her satchel, as Katie continued to stare at her.

"You're right. Sorcha isn't coming. I have to leave. I can't stay here. I got up early and came to town before she woke up."

"Why?" Katie moved closer. "Sorcha has spoken of nothing but your visit for the last few weeks. Why are you leaving?"

"I don't have to explain myself. I just came in to ask where I could find breakfast."

"Emer, you might as well give up. I may talk for

Ireland but Katie—well, let's just say she should have been a lawman. There's no way she is going to let you just leave without an explanation. Sorcha deserves better."

Emer flushed crimson at the criticism. Why did the women's opinions matter? *If they knew where you came from, they wouldn't even speak to you. You have to protect Sorcha. Leave now.* She had only taken one step when Mary spoke again.

"Emer, wait. Please." Mary looked to Katie. "Where's Daniel? Could he take over the store? I am dying for a cup of tea. Emer can fill us in then."

"No, I can't. I have to …" Emer couldn't finish as Mary glared at her. "One cup of tea and then I am going."

"Daniel, I am taking these two ladies upstairs for a cup of tea. Mind the store, will you?" Katie didn't wait for an answer from her husband. "Ella, take your pan with you. Ladies, please follow me. Emer, would you mind walking behind Mary? She is a little awkward on the stairs."

"What she means is, I am like a beached whale. I hate being this fat. It is so uncomfortable."

Despite the whine, Mary looked very happy. Her eyes crinkled as she smiled.

Emer couldn't smile back. The feeling of dread in her stomach was too much. She looked around but it was too late. She couldn't run now. Father Molloy had told her how these ladies looked out for the women who moved to Clover Springs as mail order brides. They knew Sorcha very well, better than she did. Maybe they could tell her how to tell her sister their mother was a thief, outlaw and common criminal.

Katie and Mary kept up a steady stream of conversation while the kettle boiled. It wasn't until the tea was ready and they were all sitting eating cake that the attention came back to Emer.

"So, do you want to tell us why you are running away and leaving Sorcha broken-hearted?"

Emer looked from one to the other. She could only see concern and a little curiosity in their eyes. Neither seemed the type to judge. But she couldn't be sure. It wasn't just her the truth affected. What about Sorcha and her family?

Mary took Emer's hand in hers. "Why don't I tell you what little I know? It might make it easier for you."

Emer didn't answer but that didn't stop Mary.

"I shared a room with Sorcha at the orphanage. She had been there for some years when Cathy and I arrived. Cathy is my sister. We came over from Ireland but our parents didn't survive the trip. Anyway, the nuns took us in. Sorcha showed us how to survive."

"Was it that bad?" Emer's curiosity overcame her decision to stay quiet. "Sorcha said she didn't like the nun in charge."

"It wasn't all bad. There were some lovely nuns and some bad ones. Just like anywhere, really. I was lonely. Not only had I lost my parents but I was also losing my sister. Sorcha tried her best to keep my spirits up." Mary took a sip of tea before continuing. "Your sister is the type that always sees the positive in everything. She's a dreamer. Always has her head in the clouds."

Emer twisted her fingers in her hands. Was Mary being critical of her sister? Why did she care? She had only just met Sorcha. Mary and Katie knew her better than she did. *But she's my sister.*

"Don't look so cross, Emer. I am not being critical, just trying to explain. It's how she survived the horrors of the past few years. Sorcha believes in fairy-tales and happy ever after. When she first came here... well, let's just say her expectations almost ruined things for her."

"What Mary means is Sorcha believes the best in everyone. She told us she hoped you would bring your mother with you so that the three of you would be a family. You leaving will destroy her."

Emer choked on her tea, leaving her gasping for air. The ladies fussed over her for a few minutes. Finally, she had recovered enough to speak.

"Believe me, our ma is no fairytale. Sorcha is best left believing what she told herself years ago." Emer stood up. "I have to go. I should never have come here."

CHAPTER 28

Katie watched the young woman who looked so much like Sorcha. She sensed Emer was hiding more than just who their mother was. Emer tried to appear hard but her eyes were so full of pain. Katie wanted to make it go away.

"Emer, please sit down. You can't leave Clover Springs today anyway. The train leaves tomorrow. Believe me when I say that anything you tell us will stay between us. Mary has known Sorcha for years. I only got to know her when she came to live here late last year. She is a lovely woman with a huge heart. I have grown to love her like Mary does. We only want to protect her. Like you are trying to. Let us help you. Both of you."

Katie stared at Emer, willing the young girl to believe her. Emer glanced up but then stared back at her hands. Mary went to speak but a look from Katie had her close her mouth again.

Katie let the silence continue, sensing a battle was taking place inside the girl's head. She needed to speak to someone but she was obviously not used to trusting people.

"Did you tell Father Molloy the truth about your mother?"

"Yes." Emer still didn't look up from her hands.

"What did he say?"

Emer's head shot up, her eyes lit up with temper. "He told me to show her respect. No matter what she did, she was still my ma. But she isn't. I never want to see that woman again. Sorcha was lucky."

Katie fought the urge to drag the girl into her arms. She sensed the girl would retreat again behind the mask of indifference she seemed to have mastered.

"It sounds like your ma didn't treat you the way you think children should be treated. Maybe she had troubles of her own."

"She did. Lots of them. Men were her downfall. Different faces but all the same type."

"What about your pa? Sorcha doesn't talk about him much."

"He's dead. Or at least I think he is. Ma said he was. But then Ma is a good storyteller."

"Emer, does your ma know you are in Clover Springs?" Mary spoke quietly.

"No. I didn't leave a note." Emer stood. The bitterness in Emer's tone made Katie want to cry.

Emer moved closer to the stairs. "Thank you for the tea. I understand you are Sorcha's friends. But believe me, my sister is better off without me or Ma. Coming here was a mistake."

Katie stood and moved quickly to block the exit.

"Emer, you leaving is the biggest mistake of all. Whatever your story, it doesn't matter. Sorcha doesn't care what you had to do to survive." Katie reached out to touch the young girl's shoulder. "All Sorcha wants is a real family. She's talked about you for so long. Please give her a chance. I promise, nobody will stop you leaving if you still decide to take that train."

"You can stay with me on the ranch if that makes things easier for you." Mary piped up. "I could do with some female company."

Emer stayed silent but the fact she hadn't moved closer to the door was a good sign.

"Emer, go and stay with Mary. At least then you and Sorcha can talk freely. If things get too heated, you have an escape. Staying in Sorcha's home probably put more pressure on the situation. You two are sisters but you are also strangers."

"I can't," Emer whispered. "The truth will destroy her."

"No, it won't. Sorcha may be a dreamer but she survived the orphanage. She came here and married a complete stranger and overnight became the mother of two young girls. She saved Jenny's life when she had measles last year. Your sister may not look strong, but she is. The same as you."

Katie studied Emer, watching her reaction to what Mary had just said. She saw her friend's words had hit home. But the fear was still there.

"Emer, whatever is in your history, you, too, are strong. We can only imagine what trials you had to go through to find Sorcha, yet you did. Surely you owe it to both of you to give it a chance. Just how bad can it be?"

Katie watched Emer's face, trying to read her thoughts. It was uncanny how similar she looked to Sorcha. But Sorcha was an open book. One look at her face and you knew exactly what she was thinking or feeling. Something or someone had hurt Emer so badly, she tried hard not to show any emotion.

"Twenty-four hours. That's all we are asking. Please. If not for yourself, do it for Sorcha. She deserves to know." Katie insisted.

"I can't tell her. Not everything." Emer's whisper was so low, Katie had to step toward her to hear it.

"You decide how much you tell her. But don't leave like this."

Katie patted the girl's shoulder and this time she didn't pull away.

"Why don't I cook up some lunch? Sorcha is bound

to come looking for you shortly. You can talk up here. The store will keep myself and Daniel occupied. Mary can take a nap."

"I don't need a nap."

"Doc said you had to rest more, so you take a nap."

Katie caught the smile flit across Emer's face at the banter between herself and Mary. Behind the mask, she would bet her last dollar there was a lovely girl in there somewhere.

CHAPTER 29

Lawrence sat at his desk, the papers he should be reading in a pile on his desk. She had only been gone a week and he felt like a hole had been ripped in his life.

He had spent the last few days socializing at as many events as his mother could fit in the diary. He had met countless suitable women but not one came close to Emer. The girls his mother approved of were all the same. They came from good families and were well brought-up. For goodness sake, the way his mother described them, she could be talking about horses and bloodlines.

He stood up then sat back down again. What was he going to do? Emer wouldn't be happy living in Denver. She would hate the social life the wife of a banker had to maintain. So why not go to Clover

Springs? Maybe it was time to figure out for himself what life had to offer. Connors could run the Denver office in his sleep. What about Mitchell? And Mother?

He had to get rid of his mother. Surely, it was time she went back to Boston. Maybe she'd take Mitchell with her?

A knock on his door interrupted his musings.

"Sorry, Sir, but could you sign some papers for me, please?"

"Come in, Connors. Take a seat and let's have some coffee. It's not busy out there, is it?"

"No, Sir."

Lawrence glanced through the paperwork his head cashier had brought in.

"Anything out of the ordinary?"

"There is one, Sir. The man wants to expand his store. Mr. Shipley declined the advance."

Mitchell. What was he doing making decisions? Lawrence opened the file, spreading the papers on his desk.

"What makes you think my esteemed cousin was wrong?"

Connors reddened slightly.

"Sorry, Connors, that came out wrong. It sounded like I already agreed with Mitchell. For the record, I think you have the makings of a fine bank manager. So please, take a seat and tell me why you think we should grant…" Lawrence glanced at the file, "Mr. Murphy, this loan."

"Mr. Murphy has owned a small store for about ten years. The store is always clean, well stocked and his customers rate him very highly. In fact, a number of them have been asking him to introduce more lines of stock. His current premise's lack of space is adversely affecting his ability to increase profits."

Lawrence leaned closer, listening to Connors. Why would Mitchell turn down such a client? It didn't make financial sense.

"His account has always been kept in credit. He has made many investments—small ones, but in a large number of different assets. I believe he will make a success of running a larger premises."

"So why doesn't he cash in these smaller investments and use the funds to buy the property he needs?"

"I asked him that. It seems there are some penalty clauses in place should he cash the investments in early. He is willing to do so but reluctant. He would prefer to take out a loan and pay the interest."

"He believes the interest will be less than the cost of breaking the investment?"

"Yes, Sir, and so do I. I have made some calculations and the figures add up."

"Did you explain all this to Mitchell?"

Silence greeted him. Lawrence looked up to find Connors staring at him. "Well?"

"I tried, Sir. Mr. Shipley wasn't interested."

Lawrence bit back a curse. His cousin shared his mother's beliefs. Only a certain type of client was welcome at Shipley's.

Well, he was in charge and as far as he was concerned, the only type of client he wanted at the bank were honest ones. Hardworking men who would succeed and whose business would add profit to their bottom line.

He signed the papers and gave them back to Connors. "Can you please ask Mr. Murphy to come in and meet with me? Shipley's Bank would be delighted to help him finance his bigger store."

"Thank you, Mr. Shipley."

"No, thank you, Connors. I will see to it you get a bonus as well. In fact, I want you to receive a bonus for every new business deal you introduce to the bank."

Connors beamed. "Thank you, Sir. The missus will be pleased. With another one on the way, she worries."

"Another one? Congratulations, Connors. Soon you will be needing to move to a bigger property, too."

Lawrence enjoyed a cup of coffee with Connors before the man was called back to the front desk. Taking his hat, he whistled as he left the office. He strolled past Mr. Murphy's store, seeing for himself what Connors had seen.

Mother and Mitchell would be furious to find he had extended credit to the store owner but he didn't care. In fact, if he were honest, it added to his good humor.

* * *

"Lawrence, you arrogant..."

"Careful, Mitchell. You may burst a blood vessel if you don't get a hold of your temper."

"Does your mother know what you have done?"

Lawrence stood. "I have no idea why you are so upset."

"You introduce a bonus scheme for the employees and overturn my decisions and you have no idea why..."

"What is going on? You know I will not tolerate scenes in front of hotel staff or servants."

Lawrence groaned as his mother entered the room.

"Good evening, Dorothea. I apologize for upsetting you. I am rather upset."

"That is an understatement. What have you done now, Lawrence?" His mother's blue eyes pierced him.

"Thanks, Mother. Why do you always blame me when Mitchell gets upset?"

"Usually, you are the cause. Will one of you please tell me what is going on?"

"It is nothing for you to worry about, Mother."

"Don't take that tone with me, Lawrence. You run the branch but you are not a shareholder. Last time I looked, I was. Mitchell, what happened?"

Lawrence caught the gloating look on his cousin's face. He wanted to punch it off but that wouldn't endear him to his mother.

"Not only has Lawrence overturned a decision I made on a loan sanction but he has also introduced a bonus scheme for the employees. All without consulting me."

"He doesn't need to consult you, Mitchell." His mother poured herself a drink before taking a seat.

Surprised at his mother's response, Lawrence couldn't resist sending a gloating look at his cousin.

"You can wipe that smirk off your face, Lawrence. While you may not have to consult Mitchell, you do have to ask permission from your father or myself."

"Mother, I am in charge of the Denver branch. I make the decisions as I see fit."

"Some decisions, Lawrence, but introducing a bonus scheme?"

"It makes sense, Mother. The cashiers meet our customers on a daily basis. They know what deals the clients are involved in. They see the amounts of investments and withdrawals being made. Incentivizing them to pick up new accounts for the branch makes sense."

"Yes, I agree. It does, provided they are paid only for quality leads. You should have discussed it with us first but I think your father would agree."

Lawrence couldn't resist a smile of satisfaction.

"Roland wouldn't agree to extending credit to an undesirable?"

Lawrence almost spilled his drink. What was Mitchell talking about?

"Did you check into Mr. Murphy? There was a good reason for declining the loan." Mitchell said.

"Well, Lawrence?"

"Mother, what Mitchell says makes no sense. Tom Murphy has run his Denver store for over ten years. His account is always in credit, the store is well run and he has a number of other investments. He is losing money due to a lack of space. I have no knowledge of any reason to make him an unsuitable candidate for a loan?"

"He is a freedman." Mitchell's mouth twisted into a sneer.

Lawrence stared with loathing at Mitchell as his mother choked on her drink.

"Lawrence, tomorrow you will go into the bank and tear up that agreement. Furthermore, you will close this...Murphy's account."

"Why?" Lawrence roared making both his mother and Mitchell stare at him.

"Just do it, Lawrence."

Lawrence put his drink down on the table.

"No, Mother. I won't do it."

"Fine. Mitchell will."

Lawrence didn't need to look at Mitchell to see he was gloating. He closed his eyes and immediately thought of Emer. If she could be brave enough to go halfway across the country in search of family she had never met, he could do this.

"Tom Murphy has worked every day for the last ten years to make a success of his store. You could ruin him."

"That is none of my concern."

"Emer was right. You don't have a heart at all."

His mother's eyes glittered furiously. "Do not mention that…name in my presence. She belongs on the street along with your Mr. Murphy."

Despite knowing her all these years, Lawrence was still shocked. "Mother, if you go ahead, I will resign."

"Of course you won't, Lawrence. Don't be silly. What else would you do?"

He looked at his mother, her smug, self-satisfied smile making him want to shake her. He had to get away from her. Not only her but the world she inhabited, where nothing mattered so long as you were rich and white.

"I am serious, Mother. Do this and I will never work for Shipley Bank again."

His mother looked at him for a few seconds before standing. She placed her drink on the table.

"The account will be closed tomorrow. Mitchell, please escort me to dinner."

Lawrence stood until they left the room then sagged into his seat. *What had he done?*

CHAPTER 30

Emer stared out the window in the direction of Sorcha's home. If Katie was right, her sister would be along soon. *Maybe they're wrong. She could be relieved I left.*

Sorcha arrived, her face stained with tears. "Why did you leave? You didn't even say goodbye."

"I left a note."

"I find you after all these years and all you could spare me was a couple of lines? How could you be so cruel?"

"That's it. I'm not staying to listen to this."

"Run away. I get the impression that's something you're good at."

Emer stilled.

"Hit a nerve, didn't I? You ran away from Ma. Why should it be any different here? Go on, run. See if I care." The last word came out as a whimper. Emer took a step toward her sister but then saw Ma's face. She turned away and headed out the door. It was best for everyone if Sorcha hated her.

"I'll find Ma. I am going to Kansas."

"Kansas is a big state. I told you, she moved around a lot."

"I don't believe you. I am heading over to the sheriff's office right now to ask him how to trace someone. I spent too many years wondering where Ma was. Now I have a clue."

Emer looked at her sister, standing in the middle of the room, her hands on her hips. She meant it, too.

She slouched her shoulders. What were the chances of her sister finding Ma? Not very big but if she involved the sheriff? He may have seen the wanted photos – maybe he'd see the resemblance. Ma looked more like Sorcha than she did Emer.

"You win. I'll stay." Emer cursed as her sister's face lit up. "For twenty-four hours. The train leaves tomorrow. But I am going to stay at Mary's."

The smile disappeared from Sorcha's face but Emer pretended not to notice.

Staying in Clover Springs was a mistake. The town was too small to hide in. Ma could find her. If she did, she'd find Sorcha, Jenny and Meggie, too. She didn't want their innocence soiled as hers was.

* * *

Sorcha drove them out to Mary's ranch. Mrs. Higgins came out to meet them, clucking over Mary. Sorcha and Emer giggled as the older woman berated Mary for staying out in the sun so long.

"Wasn't that long ago women in your condition stayed indoors. For good reason, too."

"Mrs. Higgins, don't you start. It's bad enough Davy wants to wrap me up like a china doll. Katie worked right up until she had Ella." At the look from Mrs. Higgins, Mary smiled. "Okay, that was a bad example. But other women do it all the time."

"Not on my watch, they don't. That's the last time you're going into town, my girl, until that baby makes an appearance."

"Yes, Ma!" Mary said testily as Sorcha and Emer dissolved into giggles.

Mrs. Higgins turned her attention to the girls. "Don't you look alike? I take it this is your sister, Sorcha."

"Sorry, Mrs. H. Emer Matthews, please meet my prison guard, Mrs. Higgins." Mary said with a look at the older woman. Emer saw the genuine affection these women had for each other. She shook the older woman's hand. She liked her. She reminded her of Ma Newmark. A tough woman with a heart of gold.

"Come on inside, ladies. I got cookies fresh out of the oven and some hot coffee to go with them. Miss Mary likes to dunk. I have some tea if you prefer something cooler."

"Thank you, Mrs. H. But I am going to take a nap. I invited Emer to stay here for as long as she likes." Mary turned to wink at Emer before continuing. "We have more space and it will be nice to have an ally. Someone to protect me."

"Don't be looking at me. Mrs. H is right. You shouldn't be driving wagons. Not on your own."

Emer glowed at the look of approval Mrs. H sent her. She ignored Mary's pout. The woman was almost due. She should be more careful.

She got down from the wagon, wishing once more she was wearing pants. Skirts hampered her movements. A giggle escaped her lips as she wondered what these ladies would think if she wore what she used to wear back in Kansas. Her good mood evaporated almost immediately. She still hadn't decided how much to tell Sorcha.

* * *

IT DIDN'T TAKE LONG to put Emer's things in the bedroom and send Mary to bed. Mrs. H set out some cookies and coffee on the table on the porch.

"You two can talk here. Nobody around to disturb you. Call me if you need anything. I am going to start fixing dinner."

"Thank you, Mrs. Higgins."

Emer added her thanks, watching the lady walk away.

"So now it's just the two of us, can you please tell me why you ran away?"

Emer played with the cookie.

"Emer, don't ignore me. Tell me. Please."

"It's best you don't know all the details. Why can't you just believe ma isn't a good person and you are better off as you are?"

"Everyone deserves a second chance."

"Maybe, but Ma wore out a whole load of chances."

"I don't know that. I only got your word for it."

Emer went to stand but her sister's hand shot out to stop her.

"Don't go storming off again. I'm sorry, I didn't mean to offend you. But think of it from my point of view. I can't remember our mother. I don't even know what she looks like. Have you a picture?"

No, but the sheriff likely does.

"You look like her. You have the same eyes and nose, although her mouth is bigger. She's taller than you. Fatter, too," Emer said her attention back on the cookie.

"Did you ask her about our pa?"

"Who says we got the same pa?"

"Emer." Shock was written all over Sorcha's face. "Why would you say something like that?"

"Heck. Sorry, but what do you want me to say. Ma isn't a saint. She isn't a bit like any of the women you know here in Clover Springs. I've had more pa's in my life than you've had hot dinners. Does that spell it out for you?"

Sorcha didn't say anything but sniffed loudly. Emer looked around her, wishing someone or something would interrupt them. This was worse than she thought.

"Granny said she was willful and prone to temper tantrums," Sorcha continued, her tone less aggressive than before.

"She got that right."

"She also said she was a dreamer, just like me."

Emer didn't like the wistful note on Sorcha's voice. Her sister was dreaming of fairytales again.

"You aren't anything like Ma. I don't know if she's a dreamer. Maybe she was, but …"

"Life wasn't kind to her. It wasn't easy being left pregnant with me. She could have stayed in Boston if Pa had married her."

"Don't you go blaming yourself. One baby on the wrong side of the blanket is a mistake. Two? That's a pattern." Emer's patience had run out. "Sorcha, you got to face it. Our ma doesn't care about anyone other than herself. You were better off believing she's dead."

"But now I know different. I can't go back to thinking that. I want to know more." Sorcha took Emer's hand. Emer wanted to pull away but sensed she would hurt her sister badly.

"Emer, I understand you are trying to protect me but I am a big girl. I'm your older sister, remember."

"You might be older but that don't mean you're tough."

"I'm tougher than I look. I didn't make it through years of living in the orphanage or traveling west to marry a stranger by being weak. I can deal with whatever you tell me, so long as it's the truth."

Emer looked at her sister for several minutes. She didn't look away. She stayed silent, waiting for Emer to make up her mind.

"Ma isn't anything like you dreamed of. She doesn't cook, has never kept a clean house and she never once told me a fairytale."

Sorcha opened her mouth but at a look from Emer, she shut it again.

"Ma tells stories. All the time."

Sorcha smiled, but the smile changed into a frown when Emer didn't smile back. "Her stories are lies, Sorcha. She wouldn't know the truth if it came up and knocked her out. She drinks too much, swears a lot, wears pants and … she owns a gun."

"She sounds amazing."

Emer groaned. Katie and Mary were right. Instead of seeing a villain, her sister had imagined Patty as some sort of hero. She had to tell her but it was going to break her heart.

CHAPTER 31

Lawrence was up early, bags packed, waiting to be moved to another hotel. He wasn't going to spend a moment longer than he had to living near his mother.

He dressed carefully before making his way to a rival banking firm. There, he ignored the curious looks of the cashiers as he requested a meeting with the bank manager. In no time at all, he had completed the paperwork and the process for moving his personal accounts to First National Bank was underway. At first, the manager had been suspicious but having explained the need for him to keep some transactions private, the man had given him a knowing smirk. *He thinks I am going to frequent saloons and other places of ill repute and don't want Mother knowing.*

Lawrence's amusement at the thought didn't last

long. If only the issues between him and his parents were that simple. He thought of Grandpa Joe. He would never have turned his back on a man because of the color of his skin or his so-called station in life. No, he wouldn't and neither would Lawrence. Thanks to Grandpa Joe's foresight, he had sufficient funds to take some time off to consider his options.

But before he left Denver, he had two visits to make. The first was to Mr. Murphy, where he presented the rather dumbstruck man with the funds to extend his store. "But Mr. Shipley, the bank already said no."

"Shipley's Bank is no longer any of my concern." Lawrence found saying those words didn't cause him any grief. He had spent his whole life trying to please his parents, living up to their standards. Not anymore. He was now free. He smiled, causing Mr. Murphy to look at him curiously.

"You can pay me back when you have the money. I know you are good for it," Lawrence said as Murphy's mouth hung open. "There is only one condition. You need to close your account with Shipley's Bank. Today."

"But Sir, my account has always been with that bank."

"Yes, I know, but believe me, it is best you close it. Today. Open an account with First National. Just like I did."

Understanding dawned on Murphy's face. He clasped Lawrence's hand. 'You be a good man, Mr. Shipley, Sir. Yes, indeed."

"I don't think my family would share that opinion. Good day."

Lawrence set off for his second visit, whistling as he walked down the road. He was free to make his own decisions for the first time in his life. It felt good.

He stood outside the door of Shipley's Bank for a couple of minutes. He could see why it had impressed Emer. It was an impressive building but it had no heart. He wanted to run a finance company designed to help people, not one motivated solely by the need to make money. Pushing open the door, he heard Mitchell's commands. Connors was arguing back, judging by the tone Mitchell was using.

"Good morning, Connors. Mitchell, may I have a word?"

"You have nothing to do with this. Dorothea told me I was in charge." Mitchell turned his back in a gesture of dismissal.

"Connors, could you excuse us, please? I need to speak with my cousin in private."

"Yes, Sir."

The door closed behind them. Mitchell turned around, a furious expression on his face. He paled when he saw Lawrence had balled his hands into fists.

"Mitchell, I swear I should hit you for what you

have done but I won't. Tom Murphy will be in shortly to close his accounts."

"They are already shut."

"Take that smirk off your face or I will. As I said, Mr. Murphy will be in to close his account. Connors will serve him. After he goes, I am leaving. You got what you wanted. You can have the bank and Mother with it. In fact, take the whole family. If I ever see you again, it will be too soon."

Mitchell burst out laughing.

"For a minute there, I thought you were serious but where would you go? All our lives we have been groomed for Shipley's."

"Some of us are capable of making our own minds up about the future we want. Goodbye, Mitchell."

Lawrence walked out of the office, leaving the door open behind him. He said goodbye to every member of the staff, from the cleaning lady on up, leaving Connors last.

"Connors, as you gathered, my time with Shipley's has come to an end. I wish you and Mrs. Connors the best of everything. Good luck with the new addition. Start a new account for the little one with this."

Lawrence passed the cashier an envelope.

"Goodbye, Mr. Shipley, and good luck. I heard what you did for Mr. Murphy. Yes, he called in when you were with Mr. Shipley. That was a good decision, if you don't mind me saying so. Mr. Murphy is a good man."

"He is also an excellent investment. Thank you, Connors. Good day."

"Mr. Shipley, where are you going? Are you staying in Denver?"

"No, Connors. I am off to visit a town called Clover Springs. After that, who knows?"

Leaving a bemused-looking Connors standing in the hall of the bank, Lawrence went outside and hailed a cab. All of a sudden, he couldn't wait to see Emer. He wondered what she would say when he arrived on the next train.

CHAPTER 32

"Sorcha, you have to sit down and listen to me. Don't interrupt. I do not want to risk anyone else hearing what I say. It could be dangerous."

"Dangerous? Why? Are you in trouble?"

"Sorcha, please be quiet and listen."

Emer took a deep breath. "Have you ever heard of the Bainstreet Gang?"

Sorcha's blank look was enough.

"They are a gang of outlaws. They rob banks and stage coaches."

"What have these people got to do with our ma?"

Emer glared at Sorcha. "Our ma is a member of the gang. You could say she's the leader but she isn't, really. She just thinks she is. Bill and Alfie are the ones who decide who they are going to rob next."

"That can't be. Our ma wouldn't do anything like that. She couldn't."

"She could and she does. She's been thieving ever since I can remember."

"Are you a member of this gang, too?"

"No, but there aren't many that would believe it. Patty Matthews is a well-known name in most sheriffs' offices. In fact, if you were to go see that sheriff in Clover Springs, he could probably show you a likeness of Ma."

Emer watched her sister's face but the girl was shocked so badly, she didn't register what she had just said.

"Sorcha, I'm sorry. I should never have come here."

"Is that why you ran away?"

Emer looked at the dirt. She didn't have to tell Sorcha the whole truth. Nobody needed to know the worst of it. "Bill Cheever, he's one of the worst members of the gang. He—well, he decided him and me...we were going to...'

"Get married. Oh, you poor girl."

Emer laughed at Sorcha's innocence. "He wasn't planning on marrying me, Sorcha. He isn't like your Brian."

"So you ran? Just like that?"

Emer heard the disbelief in Sorcha's voice. If her own family didn't believe her, what chance would she have with the law?

"I ran to a friend's house. He had some money belonging to me. He helped me get to a train station and—well, here I am."

"When did you leave? Two years ago. Isn't that what you said to me earlier. You haven't seen Ma in two years. So what have you been doing all this time?

"I got a job but what I wanted to do was become a nurse. Or at least I did. Now I don't know what I want to do."

"Why can't you work as a nurse?"

"Do you think anyone would employ an outlaw's daughter? People know blood follows blood. Ma is evil. She has a way of making people believe she is on their side. But she isn't. There is only one person she cares about and that's Patty Matthews."

* * *

SORCHA STARED at Emer's mouth, not wanting to hear the words flowing out of it. How could her ma be so different from what she imagined? She had dreamt of one day living in a house surrounded by her real family. *That's what you have now. With Brian and the girls.*

Brian warned you the reality was going to be much different from your dreams. But her lovely husband wouldn't have dreamt her ma could be that evil.

Nobody would. She looked at Emer, trying to be so brave yet her eyes were filled with hurt.

"Thank you for telling me, Emer. But you can't leave now. Where will you go?"

"I'll go back to Boston. Father Molloy might be able to find me a position in a hospital."

"You aren't going anywhere." Sorcha pulled her sister closer. "I haven't just found you to lose you all over again. Nobody in Clover Springs needs to know about Ma. We won't say a word."

CHAPTER 33

Lawrence sat on the train, staring out the window. Now that he had time to reflect on his actions, he wondered if he hadn't been a little hasty. All his life, he had worked toward a position with Shipley Bank.

What was he going to do in Clover Springs? As the train passed through the countryside, he saw a lot of ranches. Maybe he could start his own ranch? As soon as the idea came into his head, he dismissed it. He didn't know enough about horses. He'd heard some of Grandpa Joe's customers talking about milking cows, shoveling manure, cleaning out sheds, plowing fields, planting crops and all the other tiresome jobs associated with farming. It wasn't the life for him. So what was?

Maybe he could start a store? No, a town like

Clover Springs would already have a store. *You haven't even seen the town, yet you are planning on living there.* Lawrence couldn't understand the pull Clover Springs had over him.

Well, he could, but he didn't want to admit he was doing all this for a woman. Not just any woman but one who had turned his whole world upside down. She made him see things that had always existed but he had been blind.

What if she doesn't feel the same way? She is very independent. Troublesome, hot-tempered and feisty were other words he could use to describe her. She was also kind, quick-witted and intelligent.

The conductor announced the next stop. Clover Springs. He wondered how long it would be before she saw him? *She isn't going to be waiting at the station. She doesn't know you are coming. She may want you to get the first train back to Denver.*

He opened the car door and stepped onto the wooden platform, looking around him. It was a busy little town but not anywhere near the likes of Denver. He continued to get his bearings as the train whistle blew, announcing the train was leaving.

His trunk had been unloaded and stood on the rapidly clearing platform. He pushed his hair out of his eyes as he walked toward the station master. The old man was sitting behind a brass cage with a ready smile on his face, although the look in his eyes was wary.

"Looking for someone?" he asked.

Lawrence was tempted to ask if the man knew Miss Matthews but he didn't want to set the gossips talking. Plenty of time for that later.

"Could you tell me the name of the best hotel in town, please?"

"Hotel? We haven't got one of them. Are you sure you are in the right place, mister? This here town is Clover Springs."

"Is there a boarding house?"

"The saloon offers…" The man coughed at the look on Lawrence's face. "There is a boarding house not far from the station. Mrs. Sullivan runs it. She's a fine woman. Her son, Daniel, runs the store and her other son, Davy, has a large ranch outside town."

"Can you send someone over with my trunk?" Lawrence deposited some change on the counter before heading in the direction of the boarding house.

As he walked, he assessed the town's potential. It was small but expansion was evident, not least in the building work around the saloon. He tipped his hat but didn't stop as some gaudily dressed women strolled outside to watch him pass. He kept walking past a mercantile. It reminded him of Murphy's store. Smiling, he continued walking, tipping his hat at some of the town's inhabitants. The men answered his greeting while their wives blushed. He guessed they weren't used to seeing someone walking down the street dressed as he was. He should have gone shopping for more suitable clothing. He hadn't walked far past the white church before he came to the Sullivan boarding house. He was pleasantly surprised. The outside looked well maintained while the smell coming from one of the windows spoke to his now-growling stomach.

Pushing open the door, he was greeted by a teenage girl. She blushed prettily, her dark eyes dancing. Her Irish accent surprised him.

"Good morning, Sir. Can I help you?'

"The name's Shipley. Is your mother home? I would like to take a room if you have one?"

"We do. Wait a moment, please." The girl turned to call out. "Mrs. Sullivan, could you come to the desk, please? There's a gentleman to see you."

"What is it, Ellen? The cake is just about ready. Oh, my…" The older woman turned to Lawrence. "Please excuse my manners. I'm Mrs. Sullivan. Welcome to my home."

"Thank you kindly, ma'am. Your daughter was most courteous. I require a room but I am unable to tell you how long I intend on staying."

"Yes, of course. Ellen—she's a family friend, not my daughter—will show you up." Martha Sullivan gave the girl a gentle push, making her cheeks glow even more. Lawrence smiled and bowed slightly.

"Thank you kindly. Please do excuse me. I wouldn't wish your cake to burn."

"Oh, the cake!" With aprons flying, Mrs. Sullivan disappeared.

"What were you reading, Ellen? I'm sorry to use your first name, but Mrs. Sullivan didn't tell me your surname."

"O'Callaghan." Ellen colored slightly. "I was trying to study. I want to be a teacher, only Ella makes it difficult to concentrate."

"Ella is …"

"My niece, Mrs. Sullivan's granddaughter. My sister married her son. He owns the store."

"Katie?"

Ellen stopped in her tracks. "You know my sister?"

"No, not yet. I am a friend of a friend. Father Molloy."

"Oh, isn't he just the nicest man? He was supposed to visit here but he broke his leg. I wish he could have come. Emer, she's Sorcha's sister, said he was so disappointed."

The girl stopped talking as if realizing she hadn't stopped since he arrived.

"Sorry, Sir. I talk too much. It's a bad habit of mine. Mrs. Grey is trying her best to retrain me."

"Is Mrs. Grey from Ireland, too?"

"Oh, no, Sir. She hates the Irish."

He smiled. In a few short minutes, two of the townspeople had given him more information than he would have gotten in Boston in a month. Living in such a small place would take getting used to.

"Dinner will be in an hour, Sir. We ring a bell. Will you be needing anything else?"

Lawrence shook his head, taking his boots off as the door closed. He planned on lying down for an hour. After dinner, he would walk around the town to familiarize himself with the layout. Maybe he would bump into Miss Matthews. With Emer's face the last image he saw, he fell asleep.

It was dark outside when he opened his eyes. Rubbing them, he picked up his pocket watch. He had been asleep for hours. He got up, had a quick wash and made his way downstairs. Ellen sat at the table in the dining room, reading a book.

"Studying again. You are a hard worker, Miss O'Callaghan."

Ellen blushed prettily in response to his remark. She would turn heads in another couple of years. Closing the book, she stood.

"Martha kept your dinner. If you take a seat, I will go get it."

"Did the cake survive?" he teased.

"Yes, and we kept a big slice just for you. Martha

said to apologize for her absence but she had calls to make."

"It was my fault for sleeping so long. I didn't plan to."

"It's the fresh air. It was the same for us when we arrived from Boston a few years ago."

The stew and biscuits were delicious and the chocolate cake melted in his mouth. Ellen told him a little bit about the town and its various inhabitants. It was late and he was tired so he retired early.

The next morning was spent exploring Clover Springs. His initial impressions had been correct. The town was expanding. Even though there were less people around than on the previous day when the train arrived, it was still a busy place. People were friendlier than in Boston, too. He walked around the town a few times, hoping to bump into Emer but there was no sign of her.

What if she had already left?

CHAPTER 34

"You have to keep the stove at a constant temperature. Every range is different. It took a while to master this one but now I know exactly how much wood to put in the fire."

"You make it look easy."

"It is. You will soon be baking the best cookies in town. Just you see."

Emer smiled at Sorcha's enthusiasm. She really did see the best in every situation.

"Has she shown you how to roast a chicken yet?" Brian said, smiling as he stole a still-warm cookie.

"Oh, go away with you. That was a misunderstanding."

"She tried to poison us all." Brian winked at them as he headed out the door. Her sister was lucky. She had a place to call home, two daughters, and a lovely husband who seemed to think the world of her.

She closed her eyes, trying to imagine Lawrence in a home like this. No matter how hard she tried, she couldn't stop thinking of him. His green eyes haunted her in her dreams. Why had he wanted her to stay in Denver? Surely he couldn't believe they had a future together? Could he?

"Emer, where did you go?"

"Nowhere. I haven't moved."

Sorcha's eyes lit up with amusement. "I don't think it's anyone in Clover Springs who put that smile on your face. Do you have someone special? Is he in Denver?"

Emer flushed, telling herself it was annoyance at her sister's questions. "No. I don't want a man in my life. He'll just think he has the right to tell me what to do all the time. I've had enough of people pushing me around."

"Brian doesn't do that. Being single and female isn't a good mix. Particularly out here where there are more men than women. You are young. You'll find someone to love who will love you right back."

Sorcha's smug smile annoyed Emer more than her words. Why did everyone assume that the only thing a woman could aspire to was to get married? Couldn't there be more to life?

"Sorcha, I've seen first hand what love does. I want nothing to do with it."

"But don't you want children someday? I've seen you with Meggie. You're a natural mother."

Emer stared at a point behind her sister's head. Yes, she would love children but the price she had to pay to achieve them was too high. She had seen what love did to Patty and then to Minnie. Thanks, but no thanks. *What about Lawrence? You love him, don't you?*

"Emer? You okay?"

"Quit fussing over me. I'm fine. I thought we were taking those cookies into town to visit with Katie."

Hurt filled Sorcha's eyes but Emer refused to feel guilty. She hadn't wanted to discuss love, marriage and babies.

"You take them to Katie. I have chores to be doing." Sorcha pushed the plate of cookies into her hands before storming out the door in the direction of the barn.

EMER PUSHED the store door open, her mind preoccupied with the argument with her sister, and walked straight into Lawrence. Cookies flew everywhere as her basket crashed to the ground.

"What are you doing here?"

Her heart thumped loudly as she bent to pick up

the basket. He bent, too, and the scent of sandalwood soap and his unique smell brought the blood rushing to her head. His green eyes lit up with merriment as her cheeks flushed deeper.

"I would have come earlier if I knew such a warm welcome was waiting."

"Stop teasing me. Why are you in Clover Springs?"

"Why else?"

"To see me?" The words popped out before she could stop them. Her blood raced. He would think her forward and unladylike. Not that she was a lady. Oh, heck, why did he make her stomach do cartwheels?

"Emer, are you all right? Where's Sorcha?"

"Miss Matthews is a little…shaken."

Lawrence's arm gripped her elbow as he moved her toward a chair. "You best sit down and put your head down a little. It will help the dizziness."

Emer resisted the urge to kick his ankles. She wasn't some lily-livered society girl who fainted at the sight of a handsome face. *Handsome? What was he doing here in Clover Springs?*

"I'm fine, Katie, just slightly winded. I collided with Mr. Shipley."

"You two know each other?"

Emer saw the curiosity in Katie's eyes.

"We met in Boston. A mutual friend introduced us. Father Molloy."

"Shipley of Shipley's Bank. Father Molloy

mentioned your kindness in his letter. Please come in and have some tea. I don't miss Boston but I do miss Father Molloy."

"Maybe another day, Mrs. Sullivan. Miss Matthews promised me a tour of Clover Springs and an introduction to her family."

Emer held her breath. She had promised no such thing. She looked into his eyes and saw a challenge.

"It's a long walk."

"I've hired a buggy."

Emer bit her lip. He had an answer for everything.

"I can't take a ride in a buggy with you. Alone."

Lawrence raised his eyebrows, his eyes dancing with laughter and a look she couldn't interpret.

"Since when do you worry about what others think, Miss Matthews? I can assure you, your honor is safe with me. Now, do you have shopping to do or can we leave now?"

Emer didn't get a chance to argue. "Emer, would you mind taking some cloth for Sorcha? It came in this morning. Nice to meet you, Mr. Shipley."

As soon as the town had disappeared behind them, Lawrence reined in the horses.

"I am sorry for springing this on you, Miss Matthews. I was hoping you would be pleased."

"I am glad to see you. It was a surprise." Emer's heart was beating so fast, she struggled to maintain a proper tone.

"A nice one, I hope."

Emer had no intention of saying yes. "Why are you here? What happened to the bank?"

"Mitchell."

"Mitchell?" She didn't bother hiding her dislike. "Why?"

"I had a falling out with my mother. I've resigned my position."

"You left the bank?"

"Yes, Miss Matthews. Don't look so shocked. In fact, you are slightly to blame."

Emer sat up straighter. "I didn't tell you to leave."

"No, but you didn't approve of me staying, either. I distinctly remember you saying that our bank didn't help real folk. Maybe now I can find out what you meant. But first, tell me—are you pleased to see me?"

Emer looked at his face, trying to see if he was teasing her again, but he looked in earnest. *Was he blind? She was thrilled to see him. Frightened, too.*

"Yes, it is nice to see you." Emer concentrated on playing with her drawstring purse.

"Good. I missed you, too."

With a click of his tongue, Lawrence had the horses moving again. He followed her directions to Sorcha's house.

Jenny and Meggie came running as they came into view. "Emer, you're back. Oh, who are you?"

Emer watched Lawrence carefully. How would he answer Meggie's question.

"I am Lawrence, a friend of Miss Matthews." He bowed to the children, causing them to giggle.

"Are you here to marry Aunt Emer?"

"Meggie. What a thing to say?" Flustered, Emer didn't know where to look. Lawrence stood in front of her, offering his hand to assist her down from the buggy.

"Why don't you answer for me?"

Emer resisted the urge to slap his face.

"Mr. Shipley, please mind your manners."

Her haughty tone made him burst out laughing. Instead of taking her hand, he put his hands on her hips and swung her out of the buggy, her skirts flying high.

"Put me down this instant," Emer demanded as Jenny and Meggie dissolved into fits of giggles.

"I rather like holding you, Aunt Emer." He was so close, she knew he could feel her pulse racing. She looked into his eyes as he stared at hers before moving his gaze to her lips. She watched, fascinated, as his green eyes glowed darker. Everything disappeared but the two of them. Instinctively, she leaned into him.

"What on earth?"

Sorcha's shocked voice brought them all to their senses.

"Ma, Auntie Emer brought a man home from town.

He's here to…"

Emer cut off the rest of Meggie's sentence by speaking over her. "Sorcha, this is Mr. Shipley. Mr. Shipley, my sister Sorcha Petersen."

"Good morning, Mrs. Petersen. I am sorry for arriving on your doorstep but Miss Matthews spoke so much about you, I had to meet you."

Emer watched as Sorcha's cheeks flushed at Lawrence's gallantry. She put her head to one side as she studied him before turning her attention to Emer. Emer looked away, unable to answer the questions in her sister's eyes.

"Please, come in. Would you like some coffee? We baked cookies this morning."

"Yes, I'm afraid I made Miss Matthews drop her pail at the store."

Sorcha's eyebrows flew up at this comment but Emer busied herself, taking off her shawl and hanging it on a peg near the door. She put more wood in the stove before filling the pot with water.

"Emer, sit down and keep Mr. Shipley company. Mr. Shipley, please sit down. Meggie, go find your father. Jenny, have you done your chores?"

Emer didn't get a chance to argue as her sister issued orders to all of them.

She sat staring at the floor. She guessed he was looking at her as the back of her neck tingled. What was he doing here?

CHAPTER 35

"Fine homestead you have, Petersen. I can see why you picked this spot," Lawrence said as the men walked out of the house.

Brian beamed at the praise.

"You have some nice horses, too."

"My sister, Nandita, gave me some. The others I bought when Cal Sutton sent me to Denver. He told me to take my choice as payment for my services."

"Brian wants to have his own horse ranch one day. He's amazing with the animals. He seems to know exactly what they want." Sorcha lovingly looked up at her husband.

Lawrence wondered what it was like to be part of a couple so in love with one another. Emer told him they had been strangers when they married but it seemed like they had known each other forever. They may not have much compared to his parents but what they lacked in finances was made up for in love. Their simple life held so much appeal compared to his life in Boston or Denver.

Emer came out of the house, the sun glinting in her hair. She carried a tray of homemade lemonade and cookies.

"Are you trying to sweeten me up, my dear Miss Matthews?"

"Not at all, Mr. Shipley. The cookies are good but they aren't that powerful."

Lawrence laughed loudly as the adults around him joined in. The children looked puzzled.

"My sister has the makings of a fine baker, Mr. Shipley."

"Your sister has many talents, Mrs. Petersen." Lawrence winked at Emer, who blushed prettily. She had softened a bit since she'd come to live in Clover Springs. It was as if the girl was learning to trust outsiders and let them see the real person. He liked it.

"So how do you like Clover Springs?" Sorcha asked as he bit into a cookie.

Lawrence considered his answer. "I only arrived a couple of days ago but I like it just fine, Mrs. Petersen. In fact, I may decide to stay here for a while."

"Is there something in particular of interest to you?"

"Sorcha, that's enough. You are making our guest

uncomfortable." Brian turned to Lawrence. "Mr. Shipley, would you like to see the rest of my spread?"

"Please call me Lawrence. I would be delighted. Afternoon, ladies."

LAWRENCE ENJOYED the time he spent with Brian. The man was extremely knowledgeable about both the area and his horses.

"Why don't you expand your business?"

"Cash is king in Clover Springs just as it is everywhere else, Lawrence. The banks don't see fit to lend money to folks like me."

"Why not? You have the makings of a fine business. Clover Springs is expanding. Expansion can only result in an increase in demand for your services." Lawrence looked around him as he spoke. He wasn't paying attention and walked right into Brian's back.

"If only the bankers I have dealt with in the past thought like you. Did you know the storeowner, Daniel Sullivan, had to marry in order to get a loan to buy the store? He had over fifty percent of the purchase price saved, too. Now, don't get me wrong, I don't think he ever regretted marrying Katie, but still." Brian started walking once more. "Bankers aren't held in too high regard around here."

Lawrence didn't say anything. He waited until

Brian realized what he'd just said. It didn't take more than a few seconds before the other man reddened.

"Shoot, here's me shooting my mouth off. You're a banker. I didn't mean no offense."

"None taken, Brian. Emer said something similar on the train from Boston. I think the two of you may just be onto something."

LAWRENCE RODE BACK TO TOWN, his brain reviewing the conversation with Brian. He was certain in a town like Clover Springs, he would find many other potential customers facing the same funding issues as Brian. His father would consider these deals to be too high risk for the low return involved for their Denver branch. But he didn't have to consider his father's feelings anymore. He was free to do what he wanted. Did he have sufficient funds to open a bank here in Clover Springs? Was there enough business to sustain it?

He pulled up outside the stables, handing the rented rig back to the owner. If he was to live in Clover Springs, he needed to find somewhere more permanent to live. His mother would have a fit. Smiling, he pushed the door of the boarding house open.

The desk was unattended when he entered so he headed straight up the stairs. He opened his room to find his cousin waiting for him.

"Mitchell, what are you doing here?"

"The bank's been robbed."

"When?"

"A few days after you left. It took a while to track you down. Your mother sent me to get you. You ignored her telegrams. She told me not to return without you."

"Telegrams? I didn't get any. Was anyone hurt?"

"The head cashier got hit in the chest. Nothing the docs could do. The raiders didn't get much, though. Seems the staff suspected something and hid some of the cash in the second safe." Mitchell glanced around him. "Couldn't you find anywhere better to stay?"

"Darn it, Mitchell. The man had a name and a family. Don't you even care a man gave his life to protect the business?"

Mitchell's face flushed but he didn't say anything.

Lawrence strode over to the window and threw it open. He couldn't breathe. *What type of family did he come from where someone's life held so little value?*

"What did Mother do for Connors' family?"

"Who?"

"Mitchell, I could hit you right now. Connors, the man who died." When Mitchell didn't meet his eye, he swore under his breath. "She didn't do anything, did she? For the love of God, don't you people care about anything other than yourselves?"

"Don't you mean ourselves? You stand there

berating me when you are the one who decided to go chasing after some floozy when you should have been at the bank. You have no right to talk to me about priorities."

"Don't ever call her that name again." Lawrence took deep breaths, trying to gain control of his temper. "Emer Matthews is a fine young woman."

Mitchell started laughing but stopped at the fierce look Lawrence sent in his direction. "You can't be serious?"

Lawrence didn't say anything but turned to stare out the window. He wasn't sure of Emer's feelings but he wanted her in his life. He wasn't about to discuss that with Mitchell.

"Can't you just bed her and get her out of your system?"

"Mitchell..." Lawrence growled taking a step toward his cousin.

"Oh, this is rich. You've fallen for her. Your mother will have a fit. Your father will disown you. It was bad enough you resigning from the bank, but to throw your whole life away over a two-bit girl?" Mitchell didn't bother to hide the glee from his tone. He was probably already counting the riches coming his way if the Shipley family acted as he described.

Lawrence found he didn't care what they did. They could keep their money and their reputation. He would start over with Grandpa Joe's money. He wouldn't be as rich as his parents but he would be happier. Here in Clover Springs.

"Emer is worth ten of you. Mitchell, get out and don't come back."

"But where will I go? The train doesn't leave until tomorrow," Mitchell whined.

"I don't care but leave now. I can't guarantee your safety if you stay a second longer. "

Mitchell blanched before moving toward the door.

Lawrence paced the room for a few minutes before he swore. Connors had died saving their bank. The least he could do was provide for his family. The eldest was only ten.

His mother should have done something, even if she had only paid for the funeral. He grabbed his coat and headed back out. He would send a telegram to Travers. He'd look after the Connors from his own personal finances. Thanking Grandpa Joe once more, Lawrence went to find the telegraph office.

CHAPTER 36

The next morning, Lawrence was sitting at breakfast, reading the paper. Mitchell appeared in front of him, looking wary.

"What do you want?" Lawrence didn't even attempt to be friendly.

"I'm going back to Denver. Your mother..."

"My mother can go to blazes. I told her I wasn't coming back to Shipley's. I will be back to visit her when I feel the time is right and no sooner."

"Lawrence, do you think that's wise? You know how she can be."

"Mitchell, in case it escaped your notice, I am not a snotty-nosed brat running home to Ma. I am a grown man and the sooner mother realizes that the better. Now, do you mind?"

Mitchell moved to leave.

"Did they catch them?" Lawrence hoped they'd hang for what they did to Connors.

"The robbers? No but there's a posse out looking for them."

"Good. Let's hope they are more successful in their operation."

Mitchell flushed at the insult but didn't respond. Lawrence went back to his paper. Something didn't feel right but he couldn't put his finger on it. Maybe he should go back to Denver for a while, at least.

* * *

MITCHELL ALMOST KNOCKED Emer and Sorcha down as they left the store.

"Mitchell, what are you doing here?"

"As if you didn't know. I don't know what hold you got on my cousin. You remember, though, blood is thicker than water. He might be taken with you now but as soon as Dorothea pulls the purse strings, he'll come running."

"Excuse me, Sir. I don't like your tone." Sorcha took a step in front of her sister but Emer didn't need protecting.

"Never mind his tone. I don't like him. Get lost, Mitchell Shipley, and don't come back. Your kind aren't welcome here."

“If this town admits the likes of you, *Miss* Matthews, that suits me just fine.”

"Of all the rotten things..." Sorcha fumed.

"Don't pay him any heed. He's nobody and he knows it. Mrs. Shipley keeps him around as she likes having a lapdog. She'll tire of him one day. I wonder what he was doing here, though."

"Mr. Shipley is bound to know. Why don’t you ask him?"

Before Emer could say anything, the voice she dreamed of answered.

"Good morning, ladies. Lovely day, isn't it?"

"Good morning, Mr. Shipley. It is indeed a pleasant day. Perfect for a picnic, wouldn't you say?"

"I would indeed, Mrs. Petersen, especially if you were to bring some of your fine cookies."

"Emer said she would bake some this morning. We will pack a few extra. Why don’t you ride out to the homestead around noon? Brian can take a break then. Frank, too, if he’s free.”

“I’d be delighted. Thank you, Mrs. Petersen. Miss Matthews.” Lawrence bowed but his eyes were dancing with laughter.

Sorcha took Emer’s arm as they walked home. “I am growing rather fond of your Mr. Shipley.”

“He’s not mine and well you know it. Now, can we change the subject?”

Sorcha didn't speak but the slow smile on her face said all she needed to say.

* * *

LAWRENCE RODE out to the Petersen homestead, candy for the children and chocolates for the ladies stored in his saddlebags. He had resisted the urge to buy Emer a pretty shawl. It wouldn't be proper. They weren't officially courting. *What are we doing?*

He liked Clover Springs a lot. The people he had met were very pleasant. He had spent the evening before playing cards with the sheriff and the doctor.

The afternoon passed very pleasurably. He enjoyed speaking to Brian and Frank, although he sensed there was an issue between the two men. Frank wasn't unpleasant company but it was clear there was something on his mind. When he thought people weren't looking, he seemed to be watching the Indian girl. Lawrence smiled to himself. What would his mother think if she saw him having a picnic on the prairie with a freedman and Indians? It would give her a fit of the vapors.

"Mr. Shipley, is your cousin staying long in town?" Sorcha's nose wrinkled as she spoke. *What had Mitchell done now?*

"Mitchell should have left already. How did you know he was here?"

"We had the misfortune to bump into him in town. He was extremely rude." Sorcha looked pointedly at Lawrence. "He made some nasty comments about my sister. She deserves to be treated better."

Lawrence balled his fists. Seemed his cousin would never learn to stay out of his business. "I hope Miss Matthews let him see her temper?"

Sorcha smiled as her gaze found Emer, who had gone to the stream to wash off some plates. "I think my sister was the victor. I do hope your cousin doesn't come back."

"Sorcha." Brian's tone held a soft rebuke. "Lawrence is our guest."

"Your wife is right, Brian. I, too, hope that is the last we see of Mitchell. Every family has a black sheep. I wish I could say Mitchell was ours but I believe my mother would bestow that particular honor on me."

Lawrence stood up. "Excuse me while I go and apologize to Miss Matthews."

He knew Emer had seen him walk toward her. She held her body straighter, wrapping her arms around herself, as if she needed protection.

"I'm sorry, Emer."

"Why?"

"Your sister told me Mitchell upset you."

"I don't care about him. Why are you here? What business do you have in Clover Springs?"

"You."

Emer pulled back, a frown creasing her pretty face. He glanced behind him but the other adults were engrossed watching the children.

He moved toward her gently. "Emer, I think we both know you're the reason I'm here. I can't stop thinking about you."

"Don't, Lawrence. Please." Her voice shook with emotion.

He couldn't have misread her feelings, could he? *Only one way to find out.*

He took a step closer. She didn't move. Putting his arm out, he pulled her gently behind the cover of some trees. He didn't want to subject her to gossip, even if they were family.

"Emer, I've never felt like this before. You are so different from the women I met before."

She stiffened in his arms. *Darn it, that came out wrong.* "What I mean is—oh, heck." He brought his mouth down, brushing his lips gently across hers. He kissed her eyes, her nose and her lips once more before cradling her to him. "Emer, I couldn't stay away from you. I …"

She pushed him away. "Don't say it. Don't tell me you love me. You don't know me."

"True, but I know I care for you. You care for me, too." He put his finger under her chin, forcing her to look up into his face. He didn't expect her face to be frozen with fear. Instinctively, he loosened his hold on her but didn't let her go completely.

"Emer, I would never hurt you." He brushed the side of her face with his finger. With a sob, she turned her face into his hand.

He sensed she was struggling to believe him. He pulled her into his arms, trying to show her how much he cared. He held her, kissing the top of her head a couple of times until her shoulders stopped heaving.

"You and me? It's not right," she whispered.

"Why? We are both adults. Free to find love where we choose, aren't we?"

"But what about your mother? She hates me."

"Is that all? You're worried about my mother? Darling, she hates everyone, including me."

She was so vulnerable, staring up at him, her face a mixture of fear and want.

"I love you, Emer. Nobody will keep me away from you. I fell in love with you the first day I saw you when you stuck your tongue out at Smithers."

Her cheeks pinked, making her look even more beautiful.

"You saw that? Nobody was supposed to."

He kissed her thoroughly, all thought for where they were forgotten. He wanted this woman and was going to do his best to show her how much.

* * *

EMER'S HEART beat so fast she couldn't think of anything but his lips on hers. It was so good to be held by someone. She moved closer to him, not wanting to ever let him go.

He loved her. He didn't care about his mother or anyone else. Just her. He doesn't know me. If he knew about Patty he would run back to Boston. Why was she thinking of Patty now?

He broke their kiss, holding her tight against him for a couple of seconds. "We best get back to the others. They will be wondering where we got to."

She stared at him, not releasing her hold. She didn't want to go back to her family. Reality would set in. This wasn't real. It couldn't last. He didn't know who she was. Not really.

"Emer, smile. You look like you were just condemned rather than kissed."

She nearly vomited at his choice of words. *Condemned. That's exactly what I would be, if people knew who I was. Would he condemn me, too? If he loves me, he would stand by me and protect me. Wouldn't he?*

"Lawrence, wait. There's something you should know."

He kissed her quickly before taking her hand. "I know you feel the same as I do. That's enough for now. Come on, let's get back to the others."

She let him hold her hand as they walked back to

where the others were sitting. She could feel Sorcha looking at her but she didn't look up.

Lawrence gave the children some candy before telling them to go play. She couldn't say anything or look up at anyone. She resisted the urge to squeeze her eyes shut and pretend she was somewhere else.

"Mrs. Petersen—Sorcha, if I may. You asked me earlier why I came to Clover Springs. The answer is simple. I love your sister and plan on making her my wife."

Emer's head shot up. She hadn't been expecting him to make the declaration so publicly.

"I know we haven't known each other very long. I also know that you will expect me to prove myself. I have just walked away from my banking career and as yet, I am not one hundred percent sure of how I will support a wife and family."

Emer's heart jumped as he squeezed her hand.

"I believe Clover Springs will offer many opportunities. I have some means, so hopefully it won't take too long to get settled."

Emer was glad she was sitting down as her legs would have given way underneath her. She risked a look at Lawrence under her lashes. His loving look almost reduced her to tears.

Brian coughed, dragging her attention to her brother-in-law.

"At least one man around here knows what he

wants." Brian sent a pointed look at Frank before grasping Lawrence's hand to shake it.

"I haven't known Emer long but she is a fine woman. You are a lucky man, Lawrence."

Sorcha hugged Emer close. "I hope you are as happy in your marriage as I am."

The rest of the afternoon passed in a haze of celebrations. Emer sat with the others, a smile on her face but her stomach turned over and over. She couldn't shake the feeling this happiness wasn't going to last.

CHAPTER 37

"I can't believe the weeks are going so fast. Mary's baby will be here any day now and then it will be your wedding. I love weddings."

Emer smiled. She couldn't believe how happy she was. She loved Lawrence and he seemed to feel the same way.

She hadn't seen much of him over the last week as he worked hard to set up his own bank. Brian and Davy had introduced him to a lot of ranchers, all of whom were potential customers. Daniel had already opened an account and planned on moving his business from the bank he had used in Denver.

Sorcha and herself had bonded like sisters who had grown up together, and Sorcha's friends never made Emer feel like an outsider. For the first time ever, she felt she had a real home.

Katie and Emer jumped as a man barged through the door of the store.

"Where's the doc? Paul Kelley was hit in the shoulder and Jason Patterson got a bullet in his belly. He's lost a lot of blood."

"Doc is out at the Webber's place. He won't be back until tomorrow," Daniel said. "Take Paul and Jason to the doc's rooms. We'll get them help."

Don't get involved. There is bound to be someone who knows about gunshots. Emer moved slightly away from the group who had gathered—not far, or she couldn't hear what was being said.

"Katie, can you go for Mrs. Grey? She knows how to handle these situations."

"Mrs. Grey headed out to see Mary earlier this morning. Doc said Mrs. Grey was to deal with all births now."

"Heck, why did the sheriff have to bring back two wounded today?" Daniel Sullivan exclaimed, his worried look mirroring that of the group around them.

"I don't think he planned it, darling, do you? Emer, come with me."

"Me? I can watch the store for you."

"Daniel will do that. Come on, we might be able to do something."

Katie picked up her skirts, walking quickly after the posse. Emer had no option but to follow. *I don't have to do anything. I can just watch.* But a nagging feeling in her gut told her this wasn't good.

They arrived at the doc's house where a number of people were standing around the two men. Emer stood for a couple of minutes watching, but when one man cleaned his hands on his shirt before reaching to probe Paul's bullet wound, she had to act. She couldn't risk staying quiet and letting a man die.

"Stop. Don't touch him." Emer's voice shook slightly but it was loud enough to make everyone look up.

The sheriff stared at her. "What do you mean stop? I got to see whether the bullet is still in there."

"You will kill him if you touch him. Your hands are filthy. You got to wash them first." Emer looked from the patient to the sheriff.

The crowd murmured as the sheriff looked at her. Emer stood her ground.

"She's right. Mrs. Grey always washes her hands before touching a patient," Katie confirmed before moving to the sink.

The sheriff stood back. "Why don't you take over here, little missy, and show us all what to do."

Emer ignored the sarcastic tone. "Katie, when you've washed up, can you please take off his shirt?"

Emer and Katie scrubbed their hands with soap and hot water. Once satisfied they were clean, they approached the bed where Paul Kelley lay unconscious. Katie removed his shirt carefully, allowing Emer to examine the wound.

"Looks like the bullet went right through and out the other side," Emer said to the sheriff who was looking over her shoulder. The sheriff took a closer look and nodded his agreement.

"Then patch him up and we'll take him home."

"It's not that simple." Emer gulped, trying to quell the rising nausea. "His shirt is filthy. We have to wash out the wound. If any of his shirt is in that wound, it will become infected. He will die."

"Are you some sort of nurse? You don't look old enough to have any real experience." The sheriff scrutinized her closely.

Emer ignored the sheriff and concentrated on the wound. She didn't want to explain to the sheriff exactly how she came to have so much experience with bullet wounds.

"My friend's pa was a doctor back in Kansas. He let me help him. Said I would make a good doctor some day."

"A lady doctor." The men around the sheriff laughed at his tone but the sheriff didn't. He looked at Emer so carefully she had to fight hard not to flinch from his gaze. *He knows there's more to it.*

"Okay, then, Doc, what do you need to do?"

Emer ignored both the sarcasm and the title. "I need to get that piece of fabric out. See?" Emer pointed to a scrap of blue stuck deep inside the wound. The sheriff looked for himself as Emer moved toward the doctor's medical instruments lying on a mat in the room. She found what she needed. Praying hard, she held the instrument in front of the wound.

"You best stop shaking first, girl." The sheriff spoke so low nobody else heard him. "Whatever your story, it don't matter. Just do your best to save Paul."

Emer swallowed hard, willing her hands to stay still. She wasn't used to working with such an audience. She looked at her patient. He was out cold but how long would that last when she started probing the wound?

"Can you hold him still for me, please? It will be painful and I don't want him coming to at the wrong time."

The sheriff motioned for two men to hold Paul down.

"You can do it," he whispered to Emer. Taking a deep breath, she probed the wound as she removed the piece of blue material. The crowd moved closer, trying to see what she was doing. Emer fought hard to stop her stomach roiling. There didn't seem to be enough air in the room.

"Sheriff, can you clear the room? I can't do this with everyone watching."

"Everyone out. Give the ladies some space. Go on. Get."

The crowd left, muttering loudly, leaving Katie, the sheriff and Paul's brother behind watching Emer.

"We have to wash out the wound. It's going to be painful. I don't know what your doc would use but hot water is better than nothing."

"I'll boil more water. You can then use the cooled water to cool it to whatever temperature you need." Katie smiled warmly at Emer. "I'd never have guessed someone so young would be so good with doctoring."

Emer shot Katie a smile of thanks before turning her attention back to her patient. He seemed to be okay, but as she knew from experience the next few hours would tell. If infection took hold, he'd die.

She washed out the wound as best she could. She then packed the wound and bandaged it up tightly, just as Paul came round. "You best lie as still as you can. You lost a lot of blood. The doc will be back soon to check you." Paul didn't reply but closed his eyes once more.

The sheriff checked him. "He's passed out. Probably better off."

"What about the other man? How is he?"

"He's dying. Nothing we can do for a belly wound. Or are you telling me you can save him, too?"

Emer risked looking at him, seeing curiosity and admiration in his gaze. "No. There's no help for a gunshot to the belly. You know that." The sheriff agreed but at the same time, he seemed disappointed.

"Maybe I can help make him more comfortable. Where is he?" Emer heard herself say. *Why didn't I say I had to go home? Because someone got hurt.*

"He lost consciousness when we brought him in. He's in the other room."

Emer washed her hands thoroughly before examining Mr. Patterson. He didn't have a chance. The smell coming from his belly was disgusting. She sponged down his face, trying to make him as comfortable as she could.

"Can you help him with the pain?" the sheriff asked.

At Emer's look, the sheriff blushed. "Don't look at me like that. I ain't a hard man. Jason Patterson's a farmer. He was no match for the Bainstreet Gang."

A black cloud descended and Emer swayed violently.

"Is it the smell? Pretty rank, isn't it. You should go back to Paul. I'll take care of Jason until the doc gets back. Go on."

Emer stumbled out of the room. She had to get out of the clinic. She headed outside looking around frantically for the outhouse. The Bainstreet Gang were here in Colorado? Was Ma with them? Were they coming to Clover Springs?

CHAPTER 38

Emer checked on Paul a few more times before the doc came back. He pushed past her to examine the patient. Lawrence came in closely behind him.

"Emer? So it's true, then? The whole town is talking about you."

"Shipley, leave my nurse alone."

Emer and Lawrence bumped heads as they both looked up at the doctor's words. "Emer, that's a fine job you did. Looks like Paul might make it."

"Doc, the other man. He's..."

"Dying. Sheriff told me. He told me everything. There's nothing you could have done for Jason. I gave him morphine to help with the pain. He won't last much longer."

Emer felt Lawrence's gaze, but busied herself

cleaning the sparkling table. She couldn't deal with her feelings for him now. Not when her past was about to be laid open for all to see.

"Sheriff told me what you did for Paul. That man probably owes you his life."

"I'm sure most of the women would have done the same. I only washed out his wounds."

"We both know you did more than that. There are still some doctors who don't believe simple things like clean hands while attending a wound can make a huge difference." The doctor took Emer's arm and guided her in to examine Paul. Lawrence followed them.

"How did you know to get the material out of the wound?"

Emer stared at the patient. She didn't want the doc knowing she was lying. "As I told the sheriff, a friend's pa was a doctor and he taught me some things. It was him who told me how important it was to keep the wound clean. Our clothes have dirt on them and if left in a bullet hole, it can cause infection. So I fished it out."

"Have you thought about being a nurse? I could use someone with your skills in my office."

Shocked, Emer simply stared. Lawrence moved forward to stand beside her. "Nursing isn't a suitable occupation for a young single lady. You know that, doc."

"I know nothing of the sort. Clover Springs is a

growing town and I can't be in ten places at once. Mrs. Grey is wonderful. She sees to all the midwife stuff but I need an assistant. One who knows something about medicine and remains cool under pressure. So what do you say, Emer? Will you come work for me?"

At the moment, Sorcha burst in the door. "Emer, are you okay?"

Emer beamed at her sister. "Doc wants me to work with him. Me."

"Of course he does. The doc is a sensible man. The whole town is talking 'bout what you did for Paul."

Emer sobered. "I couldn't help the other man."

"It is very sad about Jason but it can't be helped. You didn't shoot him. But sounds like Paul might have died, too, if it wasn't for you."

"Sorcha, he is still very ill."

"He is but it's my job to make sure your fine work doesn't go to waste." The doc looked from one to the other. "Emer, I will expect you in the morning. Now ladies, if you will forgive me, I have things to do."

Sorcha swept Emer out of the clinic, leaving Lawrence behind. Emer looked back to find him standing at the door, staring after her, a confused expression on his face. *Would he agree to her being a nurse? What did it have to do with him, anyway?*

LAWRENCE STARED after Emer and Sorcha before racing after them.

"Mrs. Petersen, Miss Matthews. Wait. Please."

The two women stopped walking and waited for him to catch up.

"Mrs. Petersen—Sorcha—could you please give us a minute? I need to speak with Emer."

"I will wait for you in Katie's. I need to pick up a couple of items. Good day, Lawrence."

Now he had her alone, he couldn't speak. The right words wouldn't come.

"Lawrence, are you all right? You seem upset." Emer spoke, putting her hand on his arm.

Her fingers, although gentle, burned right through his clothes, setting his body on fire. He looked at her face, into those baby blue eyes, but she seemed to be totally unaware of the effect she was having on him. Could she really be that innocent?

Mitchell's evil insinuations played through his mind. She hadn't exactly been the blushing damsel in distress when Paul was shot. Instead, from what he'd heard, she'd ordered Katie to strip off his shirt as if he was a child and not a grown man. Katie was different. She was a married woman, but Emer was an innocent young woman. Or was she? He couldn't shake the feeling that there was a lot to this girl's story. More than she had told any of them.

His heart raced, leaving his breathing labored. He

struggled to gain control of his thoughts. He fought the urge to take her in his arms and kiss her senseless. Given they were in the middle of town, it would ruin both their reputations. Hers was already in question. It didn't help she was a single woman without any kin.

Where had she learned what she knew about doctoring? The sight of a naked male chest hadn't cost her a second thought. The women he knew would have swooned at the sight, as would any woman his mother deemed an appropriate marriage partner.

Almost twenty years after the end of the Civil War, there were still those who believed a nurse was on the same social standing as a saloon girl.

"Lawrence, you're scaring me now. Do you need the doctor?"

"How did you learn to do what you did in there?"

He watched her closely, noting how she looked everywhere but back at him. She was hiding something. But what?

"Emer, I asked you a question."

"I told you the day we helped the boy. My friend's father was a doctor. He taught me things."

She wasn't telling him the truth. His gut twisted. What was she hiding?

"Teaching you how to staunch bleeding is one thing. Accidents happen, but knowing how to treat a gunshot wound is a different set of skills. You knew exactly what you were doing, as if you had previous practice. I want the truth, Emer. Who are you?"

Her eyes widened with temper. "What do you mean, who am I? Who are you? Or rather, what are you trying to be? You belong back in Boston. Not here."

Emer moved but his hand on her arm stopped her. "How did you learn those skills? Was Mitchell telling the truth? Are you a saloon girl?"

He almost cursed aloud watching the impact of his words. Her face paled and he could feel her shaking under his fingers. It took him a few seconds to see how hard he was holding her. He let her go.

"I didn't mean to hurt you, Miss Matthews—Emer. I swear. I behaved like a fool."

Emer didn't speak but continued to stare at the ground. He moved closer to her but still she didn't respond. Gently, he touched her, putting one hand on either side of her face. He made her look at him. He couldn't find the words to tell her how sorry he was. Her blue eyes no longer sparkled but were dulled by hurt. She looked like a wounded animal. And it was all his fault.

He stroked the sides of her face as he played for time. What could he say to make it right? For a few seconds, she stared back at him as if trying to understand the feelings he was struggling to put into words.

With a deep sigh, she moved her hands over his and freed her face.

"Goodbye, Lawrence."

She walked away, her back ramrod straight. He clenched his fists by his side and took one step but it was too late. He had hurt her too badly and there was no coming back from it this time.

CHAPTER 39

Emer screamed as her foot caught in a bramble and she pitched forward. She landed with a bump but wasn't badly hurt. It didn't stop her crying, though. She cried for what seemed like hours. Why couldn't life be straightforward? What was she going to do now? She had lost Lawrence. *You never really had him in the first place.*

Nandita was the one who found Emer.

"Sorcha is worried about you. You were supposed to meet her at the store. She waited."

"Sorry, I lost track of time."

Emer looked up at the Indian girl, whose face looked as troubled as she was.

"I'm sorry. I didn't mean to worry her. I just needed some time alone."

"It is a man."

"What?"

"A man who causes the water to run down your face."

Emer rubbed the tear marks away, furious at being found crying. "No, I got something in my eye."

She was surprised when Nandita sat down beside her.

"Do you want to talk about this man?"

Emer shook her head. There was no point in talking about Lawrence. "Have you decided what you will do? Sorcha said you didn't know if you were going to stay in Clover Springs?" Emer asked, hoping she wasn't breaking her sister's confidence.

"I will go with my family. It is better for everyone."

"Why? Sorcha will miss you, as will the girls. They love you."

"It is best I go."

"For who? If I had children like you do, I wouldn't agree to making them live in a prison."

"The reservation isn't a prison."

"Isn't it? You cannot leave. At least not without permission."

"And you are free? I do not see women in the white man's world as free. You have to do what the man says. First your father, then your husband."

Emer shrugged. Nandita had a point.

"But it's changing. There are women doctors, scientists, authors and ..."

"Nurses." Nandita chuckled at the look on Emer's face. "If you are free, why are you sitting here crying, rather than celebrating your new job? Does your man not approve?"

"I don't have a man." *I don't want anyone but Lawrence.* "Why is life so hard, Nandita? Why can't everyone just be allowed to be what they want and do what they want?"

Nandita didn't answer but the look of longing on her face made Emer forget her own heartbreak.

"Why don't you stay in Clover Springs? Brian and Sorcha will help you. You have lots of friends who love you. A certain blacksmith will miss you." Emer nudged Nandita's arm, expecting a smile. Instead, tears filled the girl's eyes.

"He hates me. I hurt him."

Emer took Nandita's hand. "I don't know what you did but running away isn't the answer. Do you love him?"

Nandita nodded.

"Then tell him. Sorcha says he loves you and would marry you tomorrow. What have you got to lose? If he doesn't feel the same, go live with your family."

"Why can't you do the same?"

"The man I love doesn't want me. He has feelings for me. I know that much. But he wants me to be something I'm not."

Emer pulled herself to her feet. "Are you coming back to Sorcha's?"

Nandita surprised her with a quick hug. "Thank you, Emer. You have a big heart."

And then she was gone.

* * *

SORCHA WAS PACING up and down outside her house as Emer walked over the hill.

"Where have you been? I was out of my mind with worry. Where's Mr. Shipley?"

"He's gone."

"Oh, Emer. I'm sorry."

"It's for the best."

Sorcha looked around her carefully before whispering to Emer. "Were you told who shot them?"

Emer played with her skirt.

"Emer, now's not the time to play dumb. You have to speak to the sheriff."

"No."

"But Emer…"

"Sorcha, don't you see? Ma could be with them. Do you want to see her hanged?"

Sorcha fell silent.

"You don't think they will come to Clover Springs, do you?"

"What are you asking me for? I haven't seen any of them since I ran two years ago."

"Calm down. Anyone would think you had something to hide." Sorcha pulled Emer's arm. "You don't, do you?"

"I told you everything."

"Emer, I know that look. You're hiding something. What did you do?"

"I didn't do anything." But Emer knew it was time to tell Sorcha everything. She dropped her gaze to the floor.

"All right, darling. Hush now."

Emer let her sister pull her into a hug.

"You did the right thing, running away. I am so glad you found me."

"She was going to sell me." Emer hiccupped on a sob.

Sorcha pushed Emer away from her so she could look at her face. "Sell you? What do you mean?"

Emer couldn't look up.

"Oh, my God. You don't—no. she couldn't. She wouldn't." Shock prevented Sorcha from speaking coherently.

"She would. The ma you dreamed of doesn't exist. She's evil, Sorcha. I heard Alfie tell her to sell me to some saloon. She asked him how much she would get. Like I was a cow or a pig." Emer marched off, leaving Sorcha to run after her.

"Emer, wait. Don't you dare go running off again! You have to tell the sheriff. If she is that evil, she could have been the one to shoot those men. We have to turn her in."

"*WE* don't have to do anything. I can't, Sorcha. What will the townspeople think? It's bad enough Lawrence thinks I worked in a saloon. But if he knew I was an outlaw?"

"A saloon? Why would he think that?"

"He thought it was where I found out how to treat gunshot wounds. He was horrified." Emer's voice quivered as she held back tears. *She had cried enough today.*

"Lawrence Shipley is an ass." At Emer's shocked look, Sorcha continued. "Don't look at me like that. I didn't grow up in the orphanage without learning a few bad words. How on earth could he think you worked in a saloon? Just wait until I see him. How dare he?"

Emer burst out laughing. She was hysterical but couldn't stop.

"What are you laughing for? One minute he is courting you and the next, he is insulting your character. He has nerve."

"Courting me? I was stupid to think that would last. Men like Lawrence don't court girls like me. As for my character, the daughter of an outlaw doesn't have one, does she?"

"You're not ma and neither am I. What she does has nothing to do with either of us." Sorcha paced up and down. "We have to do something. Brian will know what we should do."

"You can't tell Brian. You promised."

"I was wrong. Emer, you're my sister and I love you. But Brian, he's my husband. I have to tell him. If Ma comes to Clover Springs, it could reflect badly on him, too."

Emer couldn't argue with her. She knew her sister was right, but what would Brian say?

CHAPTER 40

"Are you going to stand there all day or are we actually going to get some work done?"

Frank lifted his head at Brian's tone. His friend's anger radiated in waves. "I'm working."

"Working on driving my family apart." Brian came closer to Frank, his fists clenched. Frank put the tools he had been working on down. He had no intention of fighting Brian.

"Nandita leaves tomorrow. She has decided to go to the reservation."

"That is her choice. I cannot stop her." Frank turned back to his work.

"Coward."

Frank swung back, his temper now in full force. "What did you call me?"

"If the name fits." Brian stood looking at Frank, his eyes blazing.

"I'm not a coward and I don't appreciate you sticking your nose in where it ain't wanted."

"My sister and closest friend are behaving like a pair of bad-tempered mules with a burr in their backside. What do you expect me to do?"

"I ain't listening to this. I got chores waiting at home."

"Go on, then. Rush home. Can't leave a cold fireplace and colder meal alone, can you?" Brian took a step toward Frank, who bristled. "You know, someone once told me I was a stubborn old coot. Well, I'm guessing they never met you. You love her. Anyone can see that. So why not fight for her?"

"I would fight *for* her." Frank let his anger go. "I can't fight her."

"What's that supposed to mean?"

"Your sister made the choice to leave. I don't want her to go."

"So be a man and make her stay."

"What you want me to do? Make her a prisoner?"

"If that's what it takes. I'd rather she be kept a prisoner in Clover Springs than in Montana." With that, Brian walked off leaving Frank staring after him. *A prisoner? Darn it, anyway. Couldn't the woman see that is what she was set to become?* Throwing the tools to the ground in frustration, he ran outside and mounted Brian's horse. "Don't mind if I borrow her, do you?"

"Depends on what you bring back!" With a grin, Brian waved him off.

* * *

FRANK PUSHED the horse as fast as he could. He had to reach the Indians before they left. He was in luck. They were just breaking camp when he arrived. Jumping down, he threw the reins to a nearby boy.

"Mind the horse."

He saw Nandita up ahead. It wasn't easy to miss her. Not only was she the most beautiful woman there but she was the only one studiously ignoring him.

"Nandita, I am taking you home with me."

She turned on him, shouting, "How dare you order me around like I was your property."

"You are my woman," he shouted back at her. "I won't stand back and let you do this."

"You cannot stop me. You made your feelings clear the other night at the river."

"No, I didn't." He ignored their audience and pulled Nandita into his arms. Lowering his head, he captured her lips with his. She didn't fight but held herself in check. He ignored her response, intent on telling her exactly how he felt with the pressure of his lips. He knew the moment he won. Her body became pliant in his arms as she pushed closer into his embrace.

"About time you two saw your future is entwined."

"Chief Running Buffalo. Forgive me." Frank kept his arms tight around Nandita as he spoke to her chief. "I cannot let her go with you."

"You cannot make her stay, either. If you have learned anything, my friend, you should know a heart given freely is the only one worth having."

Frank bowed his head, the wisdom of the chief's words ringing clear.

"He has my heart. Now and always."

Frank's heart soared.

"I am sorry. I must stay with the man I love. Together we must build our future, here in Clover Springs."

"You have made a wise choice, my child. I shall miss you, daughter of my favorite sister. You will come visit me."

Nandita broke free of Frank's embrace to hug her uncle. "Thank you, Chief Running Buffalo."

Frank moved toward them. Taking Nandita in one arm, he held out the other to the chief.

"Thank you, Chief. I vow to honor and protect her and our family until my last breath."

"You will make fine children. Maybe someday, we will all find a way to live in peace together. Until that time comes, we must go."

Frank held Nandita as the tears coursed down her cheeks. Together, they watched the remaining members of the tribe pack up their things to ride into the distance.

Little Beaver led two horses behind him as he came to say goodbye.

"My father would want his wife to have these horses. I give them to you." The boy turned to leave. "Look after Ama and Salali. Train Mohe in the ways of our people."

Frank heard the plea in the boy's words.

"Why don't you stay with us? If Chief Running Buffalo agrees."

"I cannot live on charity."

"I need help in the forge. I'll train you to become a blacksmith."

"But what of the Army?"

"The Army ain't going to be looking for one Indian. What do you say?"

"Will I get to spend time with Ben?"

Frank smiled. "Of course. Davy told me you were training Ben on how to hunt and fish. He can't live without that type of training. I figure it's essential."

Little Beaver grinned before racing off to find the chief. Nandita and Frank watched them talking.

"This is a lovely thing you have done. He has always looked upon us as his family."

"Nandita, I would do anything for you. All I have ever wanted is your happiness."

"All?"

Frank shrugged his shoulders. "Well, if you are offering more, it wouldn't be gentlemanly to refuse a lady."

"Will you be my husband?"

Shock made him speechless. She stared at him, a smile curving her lips.

A couple of seconds passed before he could speak. "No lady ever asked me to marry them before."

"Is that a yes?" Nandita said amid Little Beaver's whoops of joy.

Frank swept her off her feet and carried her toward Brian's horse.

Nandita and Frank arrived back at Brian's house with Ama, Salali, Mohe, Little Beaver and some horses.

Sorcha and Emer came out to greet their guests.

"I take it we have a wedding to plan?" Brian asked, his arm around his own wife.

Frank and Nandita exchanged a look before nodding. "Nandita asked me to be her husband. I couldn't refuse."

The group laughed as Nandita pushed her groom-to-be so hard, he fell on his backside. He laughed, too, as the children, thinking it was some sort of game, dived on top of him.

Brian noticed the smile didn't reach Emer's eyes. "Take everyone inside. I want to speak to Emer," he whispered to Sorcha, who promptly did as requested.

"Emer, why don't you help me with the horses. We'll put them in the corral overnight."

The rest of the guests moved into the house, leaving them alone.

"Sorcha told me all about your ma. She also said you had an argument with Shipley."

Emer nodded, the light glistening on the tears in her eyes.

"I do not see any benefit in telling the townspeople about your ma. Hopefully, the Bainstreet Gang have moved on to richer pastures."

"But Paul got hurt and Jason died."

"Telling anyone isn't going to put that right. Sorcha said the doc asked you to be his nurse. Is that something you want?"

"More than anything."

"Anything?" Brian watched as her eyes dulled and her shoulders slumped in response to the question they both knew he had asked.

"He's made his feelings clear. I am not the woman for him."

"I love Sorcha with all my heart. So I am telling you this as a brother and not as a man. If that makes sense." Brian wasn't at all sure it made sense but he decided to go ahead anyway. "You are the type of woman any man would be honored to have as his wife. Never forget that."

Emer's eyes swam with tears. Brian coughed a couple of times before saying gruffly, "Let's get back before Frank drinks all the coffee."

CHAPTER 41

Emer held herself rigid as Mrs. Grey appraised her from head to toe. She struggled not to smooth the imaginary wrinkles out of her skirt.

"You look the part, although you are a little young."

"In case you are wondering, Miss Matthews, that remark constitutes high praise from our midwife." Doc winked at Emer before deciding he had urgent cases to see to.

Emer looked around the spotless office.

"Mrs. Grey, could you please tell me what you would like me do this morning?"

"Doc told me what you did for Paul Kelley. Sheriff said you told him off for not washing his hands. Where did you learn your doctoring?"

Emer had heard a little about Mrs. Grey from

Katie, who thought she was a miracle worker and Mary, who didn't hold her in such high regard. She knew she wasn't someone she wanted to get on the wrong side of. It was best she stick to the truth, or at least as close as possible without betraying her background.

"My neighbor back in Kansas was a doctor in the war. He was captured and interned in Belle Isle near Richmond."

Was it her imagination or did Mrs. Grey sit straighter?

"When he was released, he came home but never practiced as a doctor again. He took up ranching but he wasn't up to the hard work. His hands shook too much." Emer looked to Mrs. Grey but she seemed to be listening.

"Anytime anyone got hurt…on the ranch, ma sent them over to Pa Newmark. She sent me along with whomever it was. Pa Newmark saw I was interested in learning. He taught me what he could."

"Including how to treat gunshots?" Mrs. Grey asked, clearly suspicious.

"We had a fairly large spread. Some of the boys got a little crazy at times and had a couple of accidents. Nothing too serious, although one fella did shoot off his toe." The muscle in Emer's arm twitched as she related a story mixed with truth to explain her skills to Mrs. Grey. When she had finished, the older lady sat in silence for a few minutes.

Emer swallowed, trying to get moisture into her dry mouth. Mrs. Grey blinked rapidly before standing up.

"I guess that story is at least partially true. Stop blinking at me like you were caught in direct sunlight. We all have a past. I'm not interested in yours." Mrs. Grey stood and smoothed down her dress. She gestured to Emer to follow her. "All I care about is the people of Clover Springs. From what Doc and the sheriff say, two men I trust completely, you will be an asset to this town. Until you prove otherwise, I will do all I can to teach you everything you need to know about nursing."

Emer fiddled with her ear, not quite believing what the woman had said. She was going to train her how to be a nurse. She didn't care about her background.

"Remember, Miss Matthews, nursing is not a profession held in high regard by many. People have short memories when it comes to how well they were cared for by nursing staff."

Emer held her head up. She didn't care about what people thought. *Only one man. And he thinks you worked in a saloon. He'd believe nursing was a step up from that.*

The days passed in a whirl of hard work. Mrs. Grey was an exacting mistress. Emer worked harder than she ever had before but she loved every minute of it. She moved into town to stay with Ellen at the boarding house, as the ranch was a bit far outside town. Mrs. Grey spent a lot of time visiting Mary but wouldn't take Emer with her. "It's not proper for a single woman to be a midwife."

Emer didn't argue. She was interested in birthing babies but that could come later. She had enough to learn. The townspeople, initially skeptical of such a young girl doing doctoring, came to gradually accept her, not least because Mrs. Grey and the doc made their support clear. Every night, she fell into bed too exhausted to think. That was a good thing, as it hurt too much to think of Lawrence. He had made some attempts to speak to her but she'd cut him off. Love was for other people, not her. She had let herself become weak and vulnerable. That wasn't going to happen again.

LAWRENCE TOOK a step toward the clinic but stopped. What could he say? He cursed under his breath. He had lost her and only had himself to blame. Turning back quickly, he almost knocked over one of the town matrons.

"Please excuse me." He smiled his most professional smile, tipping his hat at the same time.

The woman stared back at him coldly.

"You, Sir, are an idiot."

Taken aback, Lawrence stared, despite it being rude.

"Sorry, I don't … well, that is to say…"

"Stop stammering. You can keep the smiles, too. I am far too long in the tooth to be taken in by false appearances."

With a huff, she marched on leaving Lawrence standing bemused. It took him a few seconds to gather his wits and go after her.

"Excuse me. Mrs. Grey, isn't it? I am afraid I cannot remember us meeting. I certainly do not know what I have done to cause you offense. I apologize."

"For what? Almost knocking me over or acting like an idiot? Or is it both?"

"Listen, Mrs. Grey. I know some people around here are frightened of you but I am not some silly schoolboy."

"Pity, as then someone could put you over their knee and give you a good hiding."

Lawrence opened his mouth and shut it again. He stood staring as Mrs. Grey continued marching up the street. She had a nerve speaking to him like that. *She also has a lot of influence over this town and you can't afford to have enemies like her.* He had a feeling he was going to regret this but he went after her all the same.

"Mrs. Grey, please stop. Let's start again. My name is Lawrence Shipley and I am rather at a loss to how I upset you. Perhaps you could enlighten me over tea?"

Mrs. Grey stared at him for a couple of seconds. Just as he thought she was about to refuse, she nodded. She walked into the newly opened café, leaving him to follow her. Now he felt like a school boy.

He waited until the waitress had served them tea and cakes.

"Shipley? Of the Boston family, I guess?"

Lawrence nodded. *Maybe she knows Mother. It would explain why she hates me on sight.*

"That would explain a lot but I expected you to have some backbone. You might as well close that bank of yours and head back to Boston."

Lawrence nearly choked. "Excuse me?"

"There you go again. Always apologizing."

"Mrs. Grey, I have upset some people in my time but never have I known such hostility in someone I have only just met. What is it you dislike so much?"

"You really do not want to know." Mrs. Grey started to rise.

He reached out to grasp her arm, letting it go at the look in her eyes. "Please, tell me."

"Emer Matthews." At Lawrence's intake of breath, Mrs. Grey smiled slightly. "Miss Matthews is a wonderful addition to this town. Exactly the type of woman we need. She's a fine nurse. Not afraid of hard work, blood, sweat or tears."

"Yes, Miss Matthews is lovely."

"So why are you behaving like an idiot? I may be

old, Mr. Shipley, but I am not too old to know love when I see it. I've seen how you look at her, yet you broke her heart."

"What did she tell you?"

"She didn't *tell* me anything. Emer has a past."

"Yes, well, then, you understand my position. Now, I must be going."

"Sit down, young man. You, too, have a past. Don't look at me like that. There are reasons why a member of one of Boston's premier families hides out in a town like this."

Lawrence started to protest but it was useless. Mrs. Grey continued to speak.

"I don't care what you say. You made a decision to leave that life behind you. Emer did, too. Whatever happened in the past should stay there."

Lawrence noticed her eyes had clouded and he got the impression she may have something to hide, too. *Next you will be thinking she's worked in a saloon, too.* The image made him smile but he choked it back. He wouldn't put it past the formidable woman to slap him. Her next words sent a knife into his heart.

"Emer's working herself into the ground over in Doc's office. Hard work never cured a broken heart. But when combined with sleepless nights, it leaves her vulnerable to infection. You stole that girl's happiness away. If you want to flourish in Clover Springs, you best find a way to put it back. I think you want that, too."

Lawrence sat, too stunned even to stand as Mrs. Grey left the table. *Emer was hurting and it was all his fault. He was an idiot and worse.*

Paying the bill, he rushed across the street in the direction of the doc's. A couple of people moved to speak to him but he shouted his excuses. He had to do this now before his nerve failed him.

Pushing open the door, he barged in. Ignoring the stares of patients waiting to be seen, his gaze focused on Emer tending a small child. He watched as she gently wiped the little boy's tears away. He waited impatiently until she finished.

"Emer—I mean, Miss Matthews, can we talk please?."

Her hand flew to her mouth as she noticed him for the first time. He saw the joy in her eyes before the pain came to mask it. His stomach churned as she turned away from him. "I'm busy."

"Miss Matthews, I was a fool. I can see that now. I will spend the rest of my life making it up to you." He caught his breath as she stilled. But she didn't turn to face him. He took a step closer. "Marry me, Emer. Please."

The collective gasps from the patients reminded them both of their audience. Lawrence was beyond caring. He watched her face, saw the inner turmoil as hope fought with pain in her eyes.

"Please say yes."

She gave a quick nod.

"Is that a yes?"

"Are you blind, mister?"

The patients laughed at the remark but Lawrence didn't care. He looked into Emer's face, her smile sending his heart into a frenzy. Taking her into his arms, he quickly brushed his lips across hers.

"Thank you. You won't regret it, I promise."

He kissed her again.

"Kindly unhand my nurse. She has work to be doing." The doc grinned as he spoke. Lawrence gave Emer a quick kiss, took an exaggerated bow in front of the waiting patients and left Doc's office walking on air.

CHAPTER 42

Some days later, Lawrence walked whistling into the building he had taken over while waiting for his bank to be built. Coughlin, his new clerk, looked nervous.

"Sir, there's a man waiting in your office. I tried asking him to wait out here but he insisted."

Lawrence pushed the door of his office open to find Mitchell standing behind his desk, reading through some papers. Private papers.

Fighting his temper, he cleared his throat. Mitchell looked like a child caught with his hand in the candy jar.

"There you are. Your clerk insisted I wait in here. Rather small deals you have out here. Can't see the attraction, myself."

"Honestly, Mitchell, that's the longest speech I ever

heard you make. The last one, too, I hope. Leave. Don't come back."

Lawrence stood with his hand on the door. But instead of leaving, Mitchell sat down.

"I don't think I will. Your father is planning a trip to Clover Springs. He insisted I travel ahead to make sure you are here to meet him."

"My father? Is coming here? When? Why?" Lawrence wondered what his parents were up to now.

"Your absence and the timing of the bank raid didn't go unnoticed. There's been talk in Boston. You have made rather a black mark on the good Shipley name. I gather he is not impressed. And then there's the laughable issue of you chasing after that girl."

"Mitchell, I warned you once before. Do not speak to me about Emer."

"I won't, but your father will have plenty to say."

Lawrence couldn't think straight. He wasn't afraid of his father but he wondered exactly why he was coming here. He suspected Mitchell wasn't telling him the full story. How would Emer react to meeting the head of the Shipley dynasty?

He chuckled at the vision that thought created. Emer would be fine. She could handle anyone, including his father.

* * *

Lawrence told Emer all about Mrs. Grey's interaction on her behalf.

She didn't get a chance to thank her personally as she had gone to stay with Mary for a week. Emer thought the doctor had insisted on it for both their sakes. Mary, as the baby was due any day now, and Mrs. Grey, as she was working too hard.

Smiling, she surveyed the clinic to ensure everything was just as it should be. She was meeting Lawrence for dinner and didn't want to be late.

Shutting the door behind her, she saw Lawrence walking toward her with Mitchell. *Mitchell.* What was he doing here? She glanced at Lawrence's face. He was real mad.

"Sorry, darling. I had an unwelcome visitor but he is leaving on the next train."

Emer looked at Mitchell, who was perspiring heavily. He pulled at his collar before he held out his hand.

"Congratulations, Miss Matthews. Welcome to the Shipley family."

As he bent to kiss her cheek, Emer took a step back. She didn't care if it was rude—she didn't trust this man not one little bit. He had some reason for being in Clover Springs. Had Mrs. Shipley sent him to bring Lawrence home?

Lawrence took Emer's arm. "My intended hasn't any time for you, either. Now do us both a favor and leave. Tell Father to stay in Boston."

Startled, Emer looked at Lawrence. *His father was coming here. To Clover Springs.*

Before Mitchell could answer, a cloud of dust marked the arrival of a group of riders.

"Look's like the sheriff is back," Lawrence said.

CHAPTER 43

"Emer, darling. Where did you get to?"

Her spine tingled, the fear making her feel sick. Bill. How on earth had he ended up in Clover Springs? They had heard nothing about the Bainstreet Gang since Paul and Jason had been shot. That had been weeks ago.

Turning slowly, she said a quick prayer she was wrong, only to face the man who still gave her nightmares.

"What are you doing here?"

Bill held up his hands showing the handcuffs. "Not really by choice, although if they'd told me my wife was holed up here, I'd have got here sooner."

"Your wife?" Lawrence exclaimed loudly. Emer had lost the ability to talk.

"Didn't she tell you? We got married a couple of

years back. Then she up and left me, taking a load of cash with her. But that's all water under the bridge now, darling, isn't it? These last few weeks, you have more than made up for it."

Emer groaned.

"Weeks. What do you mean?" Lawrence looked confused and angry.

Bill sent her an evil glare before turning to Lawrence. "You the banker fella she's been making eyes at? Nice suit. My Emer always did like the nicer things in life. Didn't you, darling?"

"I am not and never was your darling."

"Lover's tiff. She's fine to look at but a bit moody. She's a real asset, though. In our business, it helps to have someone on the inside."

"Mr. Cheever, are you trying to accuse Miss Matthews of some wrongdoing?" The sheriff's voice boomed out for everyone to hear. Silence descended immediately. Emer's heart was beating so loud, she thought everyone could hear it. But nobody was looking at her. They were all staring at Bill.

"Yes, Sir. But you called her by the wrong name. She's a paid-up member of the Bainstreet Gang." At the infamous name, the group of people gathered all started talking at once. The sheriff appealed for silence. Bill's voice rang out clearly. "Emer Cheever has been helping us the whole time. How else did we know when the Denver bank was at its most vulnerable?"

The crowd started muttering. But Bill wasn't finished. "She's been working with us since she got back from Boston. Haven't you, Mrs. Cheever?"

"Don't call me that. I am not yours and never was." Emer spat back at Bill before turning to Lawrence. "Please tell me you don't believe him. I wouldn't do something like that."

"But you do know this man?"

Emer looked down at the ground, her fingers twitching at her side. "Yes, I know him."

"Course she knows me. I told you. We were part of the same gang. We rode together, ate together and slept together."

Emer tried not to look at Bill but something drew her to him. Seeing the look on his face, she turned her attention back to the sheriff. He looked uncomfortable.

"Were you a member of the Bainstreet Gang?"

"Yes." Emer swallowed hard at the look on Lawrence's face. "But not by choice. Ma made me do stuff. Act as lookout, clean and cook for the gang. But that's it. I didn't do any of the rest of the things."

"Are you saying you have never stolen anything, Miss Matthews or Cheever? Whatever your name is?"

Emer stared at the sheriff. She couldn't lie but how could she tell the truth?

"Of course she hasn't, Sheriff. Emer's my sister, not some common thief." Sorcha's support, while welcome, only made Emer realize she had to confess. It was time to come clean about where she had come from.

"Actually, I did steal some money. Once." Emer spoke softly, her whisper barely audible over the noise of the crowd. "I stole some money from my ma the night I ran away. From him."

"See, I done told you she was a thief. She only ran as she knew when I caught up with her, I would tan her hide before I took her to my bed. But then you enjoyed that part, didn't you, my little tiger? Always was feisty."

The crowd took a collective gasp. Emer walked over to Bill and slapped him across the face. "You lying toad."

"He's not a liar. I was a witness. I couldn't tell you, Lawrence. I didn't have anyone to back up my story. You wouldn't have believed me anyway."

Emer looked towards Mitchell. *Why was he saying she stole from the bank?*

"I'm sorry, Miss Matthews, but I have to place you under arrest. Bank robbery is a serious crime." The sheriff wouldn't meet her eyes. He had an uncomfortable look on his face.

"She can share my cell, Sheriff. We got a lot of catching up to do, don't we, Mrs. Cheever?"

"Stop calling me that." Emer snapped at Bill before looking for Lawrence. He had already turned his back and was walking away down the street.

Emer let the sheriff put the handcuffs on her. Sorcha tried to hug her but it was awkward. "I'll get you out of here. Don't worry."

Emer knew her sister meant well but what could she do? She was, by her own admission, a member of a gang of outlaws. That in itself was enough to warrant jail time. She was innocent of the other charges but who was going to take the word of an outlaw? Especially when a rich man was one of the people accusing her?

CHAPTER 44

"Lawrence, you've got to help Emer. You know she isn't capable of robbing a bank."

Lawrence didn't look up. "I know nothing of the sort. It's obvious your sister has been lying about her past. Goodness knows what crimes she's involved in."

Sorcha cringed at the cold tone. He was distancing himself from the woman he had professed to love just days before.

"Crimes. You know she's innocent of everything but trying to get away from our ma and her gang of thieves." Sorcha tried to keep her tone calm. Getting annoyed with Lawrence wasn't going to help Emer. She had only found her sister. She wasn't about to let her rot in jail.

"Emer admitted to stealing. You heard her. The whole town heard her."

Sorcha counted backwards from ten in Irish just as her Granny had always told her. She wouldn't be helping Emer if she slapped Lawrence. "Emer didn't rob the bank. It's not the same thing as stealing. She said she took money from Ma to get away. You saw Bill. Patricia wanted to give Emer to him. You'd have helped her steal to get away from him. Wouldn't you?" Sorcha noticed he wouldn't meet her gaze. "Come, now, Lawrence. You've got to believe her. And help me to prove her innocence."

"Even if I did, just how do you think we could do that?"

"There has to be a way to help her. There must be people back in Kansas who remember her. What about Patricia? Can you hire someone to find her?"

"Like who?"

"I don't know. A US Marshall or something." Sorcha wanted to shake him. He was rich and powerful. He must know people. "Why would Mitchell turn against Emer? Bit suspicious he didn't mention anything to you before, isn't it?"

Sorcha saw she'd got his attention.

"That's a good question, one I need to find out the answer to. Why don't you go back to your family, Mrs. Petersen, and I will go speak to my dearest cousin."

Sorcha would have loved to see that confrontation

but she didn't want to get on the wrong side of Lawrence. Her sister needed his help. She walked with Lawrence back to Main Street. She went toward the store, leaving Lawrence heading in the direction of the boarding house.

* * *

"Leaving already, dear cousin?" Lawrence drawled as he walked into his cousin's room. He saw the panic in Mitchell's eyes before the disdainful look he was getting used to took over.

"Surprised to see you here, Lawrence. I thought you would be down in the jail, comforting your outlaw lady friend. Did her husband throw you out?

"Emer's not married and she's no outlaw."

"That is up to the Judge to decide, now, isn't it? Pity I won't be here to see it but I have to get back to Denver. Duty calls."

"Don't you mean my mother is calling?" Lawrence allowed himself a tiny spark of satisfaction at Mitchell's reaction. "I don't think the sheriff will allow you leave."

Mitchell paled. For the first time, Lawrence saw his cousin's forehead was sweaty. He glanced down to see Mitchell wiping his hands in his trousers.

"Of course I am free to go. I haven't done anything?"

"Yet you are behaving as if you have. What did you do, Mitchell?"

"Nothing. I haven't done anything. Now if you'll excuse me, I've got a train to catch."

Lawrence moved toward Mitchell, who backed up until he couldn't go any further.

"What exactly did you see Miss Matthews do?"

Mitchell's eyes darted from left to right but before he could answer, there was a knock at the door.

"Mr. Shipley, the sheriff would like a word with you."

Both men moved to the door but Mitchell put his hand on Lawrence's arm. "Given this is my room, I assume the clerk is looking for me. Close the door on your way out. There's a good fellow."

Lawrence itched to hit his cousin but he'd moved too quickly. It wouldn't do Emer any good if he got arrested, too. He had to do something. Sorcha had mentioned getting the US Marshalls involved. He wasn't sure that was a good idea. But maybe hiring a Pinkerton was. A detective could find people from Emer's past and prove her innocence. *If she was innocent.*

CHAPTER 45

Emer sat on the edge of the dirty mattress. The jail was depressing but it was worse knowing Lawrence believed her to be guilty. She'd seen the look in his eyes when Bill announced she had shared his bed.

Bill. How she hated that man. She didn't have to share his cell but it was directly across from hers. He spent the day staring at her. She didn't look back, not wanting to give him any encouragement. After some hours, the sheriff came in and opened her cell door.

"Come with me, Miss Matthews."

"Her name ain't Matthews. It's Mrs. Cheever."

They both ignored Bill as they walked out to where the sheriff's desk was. The doctor and Paul Kelley stood there waiting.

"Take the cuffs off her."

The sheriff did as the doctor said and released Emer. She stood, rubbing her painful wrists.

"The doctor here is accepting full responsibility for you. It ain't right, you being held in a jail cell with no privacy. Even if you are guilty of being an outlaw."

Emer swallowed hard. The sheriff thought she was an outlaw, too. She held her breath. She wasn't going to cry or show any weakness. She thought the people of Clover Springs knew her but she was just poor Emer Matthews.

"You got to stay in the doc's house until the judge gets here. Will be a week on Friday. Don't get any ideas, Miss Matthews. If you try to escape, my men will shoot to kill. Clover Springs don't need the rest of the Bainstreet Gang visiting our town."

"Sheriff, that's enough. Nobody will make me believe Miss Matthews is guilty as charged. She didn't have to admit to being a member of the gang and from what I heard, she had little choice." Paul Kelley coughed as if he wasn't used to speaking so much.

"This lady has done nothing but good things since she came to this town. I wouldn't be alive today if it weren't for her."

Emer sent Paul a look of gratitude before turning her attention back to the sheriff.

"Okay, Miss Matthews. I need your word you won't try to escape."

Emer opened her mouth but she couldn't say anything.

"Give the girl a break, Sheriff. *We* both know she isn't to blame for that gang. Come on, Emer, we got work to do. You may be wishing you were back in that cell. My office needs scrubbing from top to bottom."

CHAPTER 46

"If I'd known watching a criminal would mean a table load of cookies and cakes, I'd have done it long ago." The doc winked at Emer but she couldn't smile back. Time was passing and there was no way to prove she was innocent.

She racked her brains trying to reason why Mitchell would frame her. He couldn't know any of the Bainstreet Gang. Bill and the rest had never been east. She'd known Connors had died but she didn't know it was the Bainstreet Gang who murdered him. She cried a few tears for Connors, the kind man who had made her coffee that first day at the bank. He'd thrown Mitchell out of the office, too. *That was it.* Connors had suspected Mitchell of something. Lawrence would know. Connors must have told him.

"Doc, can you get a message to Sorcha for me? I need to see her."

"One of the ladies is due to call today. They haven't missed a day yet. I hope its Mrs. Higgins. Don't say a word but her pies are the best I've ever tasted." The doc rubbed his stomach.

"Doc, find Sorcha. She needs to get a message to Lawrence."

"Who? Oh, you mean Mr. Shipley. He isn't here, Emer. He hasn't been seen since the day after they brought in Cheever."

Emer slouched back on the chair. So, it was true. Lawrence wasn't coming back. He must believe Bill.

"Emer, you're very pale. Don't fret, lass. There is no way I am letting any judge lock my best nurse up."

"You know that's not what they'll do. Murder and armed robbery are hanging offenses, Doc. Everyone knows that."

Doc didn't answer. He sat down, too, not touching the cookies on offer. Emer put her head in her hands.

CHAPTER 47

The judge banged his gavel again. The noise in the room died down.

"Please call your next witness."

"I call Harvey Newmark to the stand."

Emer couldn't believe her ears. Harvey was here. In Clover Springs. She stared at him as he walked up to the chair. He hadn't changed much, still tall and lanky although he had filled out some.

"Please state your name for the record."

"Harvey Newmark." Harvey shuffled his hat from one hand to the other.

"Do you know any of the defendants?"

"Yes, Sir. I know the two of them. Bill Cheever and Emer Matthews."

"Emer Matthews. Is she Bill's wife?"

Harvey's stunned look made a couple of people laugh.

"Emer marry Bill? Not likely!"

"Is that a yes or a no, Mr. Newmark?"

"Sorry, Your Honor. No, Sir, Emer would never marry Bill. She hated him. He was the reason she left Kansas and went looking for her sister. Not sure why she ended up here, though. Or how he found her again."

"Mr. Cheever said he married Miss Matthews some years back. Together, they have been robbing banks and stages. They were planning the latest in Clover Springs."

"Well, I don't know what Bill has been up to. He always was a wrong 'un, as my ma used to say. But Emer?" Harvey turned to look directly at her.

She tried to smile but she couldn't move.

"She's a good gal. She didn't have nothing to do with that gang when she was a kid. Can't see her being involved with them now."

"Why are you so sure she never married Bill, Mr. Newmark?"

Harvey shuffled his hat a couple of times more.

"Answer the question please, Mr. Newmark."

"Sorry, Your Honor. Well, I guess because when I asked her to marry me, she told me she wasn't ready to get married. She was only fifteen then and wanted to find her sister."

"When you knew Miss Matthews, was she involved with the Bainstreet Gang?"

Harvey looked uncomfortable. Sweat glistened on his brow as his eyes darted around the room. "Well, I guess she was."

A loud murmur erupted in the court room causing the judge to bang his gavel a few more times. "Order. Anyone else speaks out of turn and I will have you thrown out."

"Mr. Newmark. Was she a member or not?"

"She was only fifteen and didn't have anywhere else to go. Her ma, Patty Matthews, was a real hard woman. Emer worked night and day to please her but no matter what she did, it was never good enough."

"Thank you, Mr. Newmark."

"Look, Your Honor, if Emer were a member then she didn't have no choice in the matter. Her ma made her do things. That's why she ran away. Her ma was going to give her to him. He's more than twice her age but that didn't matter to her ma. Patty never cared about no one but herself."

Emer tried to wipe the tears from her face but her cuffed hands made it difficult

"Your honor, the witness has just established the woman is an outlaw. Now, can we move on?"

Emer swayed. She dug her nails into her palms, hoping the pain would focus her. She couldn't faint in front of the judge. She didn't think he would approve of swooning ladies.

"My girl is innocent of all charges." Silence fell as a shabby and obviously ill woman pushed her way to the front of the room.

"And who might you be?"

"Patty, I mean Patricia Matthews." Before anyone could stop her, Patty spat at Bill Cheever. "You dirty dog. You ran out on us after that last job went wrong. Alfie died."

"Mrs. Matthews, please take the stand."

All eyes were on Patricia as she hobbled towards the stand.

"Do you, Mrs. Matthews, swear to tell the truth and nothing but the truth so help you God?"

Patricia put her hand on the Bible hesitantly as if afraid the good book would burn her. She whispered, "I do."

"Please speak up," the judge admonished her.

Patty cleared her throat. "I do, Sir, but it's Miss, not Mrs. I ain't never been married but I got engaged. He died. All his fault." The court laughed but quickly quieted down when the judge hit the gavel. He looked sternly at the witness.

"Please just answer the question you are asked, Miss Matthews." The judge looked sternly at the witness over his glasses.

"Yes, Sir. Or at least, I'll try. I don't remember

everything so good now. But I can tell you my girl wasn't part of the gang. She washed, cooked and cleaned for us but she didn't take no part in any raids. She was only there because of me. She wasn't married to him, neither. She hightailed it off the Half Circle as soon as his attentions turned serious."

"Thank you, Miss Matthews."

"I ain't finished. You got to let her go. She has a chance at a new life, a happy life. You can't lock her up when the only thing she did wrong was have a ma like me. Put me in your jail, but let her go."

"And would you like us to let Bill Cheever go, too?" The prosecution attorney sneered.

Emer took a step forward but the hand on her elbow restrained her. She looked up into the green eyes that frequented her dreams every night. *Lawrence.*

"Heck, no. You should hang him from the nearest tree. That's what he deserves after what he's done." Patricia took a deep breath. "He's the one who made that Mitchell guy hand over the plans for the banks. He threatened to take him on a trip and he wasn't planning a picnic. If you get my meaning."

Emer stared at Mitchell, who couldn't look back at her.

THE ROOM ERUPTED with everyone speaking at once. The lawyer acting for Emer shouted loudest. "Your Honor, you must let Miss Matthews go at once. It's obvious she's the innocent party here."

The judge agreed and Emer was set free, but she didn't leave the courtroom. Some men stepped forward to arrest Mitchell Shipley. Not only had he been involved in the raid on the Denver office but he was wanted in Boston on a number of charges, including fraud.

"Mother will be so proud," Lawrence whispered into Emer's ear as he held her close. She couldn't believe she was free and he was back.

"Lawrence, can we leave now?"

"Sorry, Miss Matthews, but you need to take a seat. You may be called as a witness."

Emer sat, her hand gripping Lawrence's so tightly it turned white. She didn't look at her mother but stared at the judge.

The trial didn't last long. They were both found guilty. Cheever was sentenced to hang. The judge seemed to take pity on Patty. He could have sentenced her to be incarcerated at the newly built women's penitentiary in Canon City. Instead, he ordered she be confined at Clover Springs until such a time as she was well enough to be moved to the female penitentiary.

As the crowd dispersed, Emer sat. She had tried to stand but her legs wouldn't support her.

Kneeling in front of her, Lawrence took her hands in his.

"You're freezing."

"You came back." Emer squeezed his hands. "You came back."

"I only left to help you. I had to find Patty. I'm sorry I was gone so long. I couldn't bear the thought of you being stuck in the jail." Lawrence's teeth gritted together as he almost spat out the words. "With him."

"I didn't stay in the jail. Doc took me to his house. Paul and him convinced the sheriff I wouldn't run. I was tempted, but I didn't."

"Thank God, you didn't. If you had, they would have hunted you down like a real criminal."

"I am a criminal. I was a member of their gang."

"No, you weren't. You were a child with a thief for a mother. You are no more a criminal than I am a farmer."

Emer giggled nervously.

"Are your knees getting sore?"

"Yes, Miss Matthews, which is why you need to answer this question quickly. I know I asked you before but I wanted to do it properly. Miss Matthews, will you marry me?"

"Oh yes, Mr. Shipley. I will."

"About time, too. You guys really know how to

keep folks waiting. We've a party to get to. The whole town is out celebrating my nurse returning to duty."

"I'm sorry, Doc, but no wife of mine is going to be a nurse. She'll stay home and make pies and cookies. Ouch. What did you do that for?" Lawrence rubbed his shin. "I was only joking."

Emer put her hand up to her mouth but she didn't get a chance to apologize.

"Emer Matthews, as God is my witness, I swear I will never stop you from being who you were meant to be. I love you."

As they kissed, the only sound was a loud grunt from the doctor. "Guess I best go tell the party makers the guests of honor have been held up. Not for too long, though. That's a respectable woman you got in your hands, boy.

Lawrence and Emer looked at one another before erupting in happy laughter.

CHAPTER 48

"Sheriff, can I have some time with Patricia—sorry, Patty, please?"

"Doc's in with her. Go in when he's finished."

Sorcha sat on the chair waiting. She looked around the walls at the wanted posters. Emer had been right. Patty's face could be decorating the wall of some jail. *Wonder if any of these men are my pa?*

"Sorcha, you can go in now. She's very weak." Doc gave her a sympathetic look on his way out.

Sorcha counted backwards to try to calm her roiling stomach. She wished Emer was here with her, but her sister said she'd never speak to their ma again. Brian would have come but she didn't think Patricia would speak freely in front of a stranger. That was rich. She was just as much a stranger to the woman in the cell.

She walked slowly, her nose wrinkling at the smell. She didn't want to identify the odors. Patty was lying on the mattress. It looked like she was asleep. Disappointed, Sorcha turned to leave.

"You look just like your pa. He had hair like yours. Used to curl around his collar when it got long."

"Where is he? Is he still alive?" Sorcha hated the hopeful note in her voice but she couldn't help it. She wanted—make that needed—to know where she'd come from.

"How would I know? I took off when I found out I was carrying Emer."

"So, we did have the same pa. What was he like?"

"He could charm the honey from the bees. He had such a lovely accent. He was British. Your Granny never forgave me for that."

"Granny knew my Pa?"

"Of course she knew him. Didn't she tell you? She hated him, though. Not only was he English but he was a protestant. He'd never been to Ireland but that didn't stop my mother from blaming him for the famine. Like he was personally responsible for killing all those people."

"Where did you meet?"

"He was the son of the family I worked for. Ma got so mad when she found out I was pregnant. She dragged me with her to see the master of the house despite me begging her not to. William's father laughed in our faces. He threw ten dollars at us and threatened to call the soldiers if we didn't leave. "

"What about William? Did he not tell his family you were in love?"

Patty sounded like she was laughing before it turned into a hacking cough. "You are a real romantic, aren't you? William didn't love me. Not really. He just wanted what every man wants. Once he got it, he didn't want to know."

"So you gave me to your mother?"

"Ma insisted. I was going to take you away, pretend I was a widow or something but Ma wouldn't hear of it. She said it was impossible for an Irish girl like me to work and earn enough to keep a family. "

"But if you knew he didn't love you, how did you fall pregnant with Emer? I thought you said we had the same father."

"You do." Patty didn't look at Sorcha. She closed her eyes. "You were six months old. You were such a pretty little thing. Even back then your hair was the color of gold. People said you looked like an angel. Ma kept telling me to leave you with her and go away. Somewhere people didn't know me so I could start again. I could get married and be respectable." A horrible cough stopped Patty from talking for a little while. Sorcha stood up. "I will be back in a minute. I'm going to ask the sheriff to make some tea."

"He's not going to do that for the likes of me."

"No, but he will for me." Sorcha called for the sheriff to come and let her out of the cell. He didn't have tea but after some persuasion he agreed to make them coffee. Sorcha carried two cups back to the cell. Patty seemed to have fallen asleep for real this time.

Sorcha sat on the chair the sheriff had kindly provided. Over the rim of her cup, she studied the woman lying in front of her. For as long as she could remember, she had dreamed of having a real mother. But in her dreams the woman had been kind with a beautiful smile. Sorcha closed her eyes, remembering the feelings she had when she dreamed the woman came back to the orphanage to collect her and bring her to a real home. But she had never come.

All these years, Sorcha had wondered what she had done to make the woman who had given birth to her hate her so much. If she was to believe what Patty said, she hadn't hated her. She'd loved her. She'd wanted her. It was Granny who had kept them apart.

Well, she would blame the old woman wouldn't she? It wasn't like granny is here to defend herself.

The sheriff came to check on her some time later. "Mrs. Petersen, it doesn't look like Patty is going to be much company for a while. Why don't you go home and come back tomorrow?

Sorcha looked at the old sheriff, expecting to see censure and judgment in his gaze. Instead, she saw understanding and concern. The unexpected emotions caused the tears that had been threatening since Patty's revelations to fall.

"Come on now, Mrs. Petersen. You know I can't abide emotional women. You get yourself home to your lovely family. Leave the trouble this one brings where it belongs. In the past."

Sorcha couldn't answer. Her emotions were all jumbled. All her life, all she wanted was to see her mother and have a real family. She had a fantastic sister. Although they hadn't got off to the best of starts, now she and Emer were as close as any family could be. After meeting Emer and hearing her story, she had grown to hate this woman. After hearing Patty's version of the story, she didn't hate her so much. She felt sorry for her.

She had to find Emer. Surely, once her sister knew the truth, she would forgive Patty, too. Maybe they could find time to become the family she had dreamed of.

She found Emer talking to Reverend Timmons about her wedding. "Sorcha, where were you? Reverend Timmons has agreed to marry us next Saturday. Lawrence has gone to send a telegram to his parents. I think he's wasting his money."

"That's wonderful, Emer. I'm so happy for you." Sorcha gave Emer a big hug. "Maybe Ma will be well enough to come, too."

Emer stiffened and withdrew from Sorcha's

embrace, staring at her as if she had lost all sense of reason.

"That woman is not coming anywhere near my wedding."

"Emer, you can't mean that. She saved your life."

"She didn't do that for me. She had a grudge against Cheever for killing her boyfriend. That's why she wanted him convicted."

"I know she hurt you but she's changed, Emer. It wasn't her choice to leave me with Granny. She said Granny made her go."

"She would say that. How are you going to check? Hold a séance and speak to Granny." Emer's eyes glittered with anger. Her tone was disbelieving. "After everything I told you about her and you still swallow her lies."

"Emer, she's our ma. She deserves a chance."

"She doesn't deserve anything. Excuse me. I have a wedding to plan. If you want to spend time with Patty, then you go see her." Emer marched off but then came back to where Sorcha was standing. "Don't get any ideas. If you try to bring her to the ceremony, I will pay someone to throw her out."

"Miss Matthews, that's no way to speak…"

"Reverend, I don't mean to be rude but stay out of this. It's got nothing to do with you if my sister is determined to get herself hurt." Emer whirled around to face Sorcha once more. "That woman you want so badly for your ma is evil. "

Sorcha stood staring after Emer as she marched down the street. Reverend Timmons coughed as if he was about to say something but she didn't wait to find out. Lifting her skirts she ran toward the store where Brian had said he'd wait.

EMER MARCHED SO HARD she had to stop to take a breath. Of all the things Sorcha could ask, she had to go and ruin her day by telling her to go visit Patty. As far as she was concerned, if she never saw her ma again it would be too soon.

She did come back and her testimony saved you and put her in jail. Emer didn't want to admit the truth. She kept walking until she walked right into Lawrence.

"What's got you all riled up?" Lawrence asked, taking her hand.

"Sorcha. She wants ... you won't believe what she wants."

"Why don't you take a deep breath and tell me?" He pulled her close and planted a chaste kiss on her forehead before taking her arm. They walked in the direction of the store.

"Sorcha thinks I should visit Patty. Doc doesn't give her long."

"What do you think? "

"I think if I never saw her again, it would be too soon."

"If she dies, will you regret not seeing her if only to ask if she's sorry?"

"For what? Having me or trying to sell me?"

Lawrence stopped walking. He drew Emer closer and put his hands either side of her head. "Darling, if it wasn't for Patty, we wouldn't be getting married."

Emer bit her cheek. That was true. She hadn't thought about her and Lawrence.

"The woman made mistakes, no doubt about that. " He wrapped his arms around her.

"Lawrence, we are standing in the middle of the street."

"Who cares?" He brushed his lips against hers. "Emer, I love you and will support you, now and forever. But, you wouldn't be the woman you are if it wasn't for what Patty did. She was wrong. But you survived. You did more than that. You thrived. You are the most passionate, bravest woman I have ever known. Don't let anything change that. If you go and see her now, you wont ever have any regrets when she's not here anymore."

"That's the longest speech you have ever made." Emer teased him, allowing herself some time to master her emotions.

"Think about it, all right? And for goodness sake, don't let this come between you and Sorcha. It took you long enough to find each other."

CHAPTER 49

The next day, Sorcha headed back to the jail cell. She had a basket of treats for her mother. Pushing the door open, she saw Patty was sitting up, alone in her cell. The sheriff accepted the apple pie Sorcha had made for him with a smile. He opened the cell and ushered her inside. Sorcha gave Patty the basket, noting what looked like tears in the older woman's eyes

"You came back." Her voice was weaker than yesterday.

"You were in the middle of telling me our history. Then you fell asleep. I want to know more. "

"Do you believe me?"

Sorcha wasn't sure how to answer that. She had believed her but then the talk with Emer had cast doubts in her mind.

"I can see you are struggling with it. That's understandable, I guess. You don't know me and I don't think your sister would have much good to say about me. Don't argue. I deserve it. I was wrong to keep Emer. I should have left her at the orphanage, too, especially as I hated her from the start.

Sorcha stopped breathing, or at least it felt like that.

"I know how that sounds but I never wanted her. She wasn't you. You were my baby. Born of real love."

"But you said our pa was the same."

"He was."

"So how can you say you hated Emer but wanted me?"

"I loved your pa and would have done anything for him when I got pregnant with you. I believed his lies. I thought we would run away and get married. Even after he dumped me when I was carrying you, I convinced myself he was weak. It was only because of his family. I was wrong. "

Sorcha stayed silent. She didn't know what to say.

"I went to your pa for help. I told you I didn't want to leave you with my ma. I wanted to go away with you but to do that I needed money. Your pa had married someone else by then. I thought he'd done it to get back on his father's good side."

An ugly sounding laugh turned into a hacking cough. Sorcha went over to her mother and held her as the cough shook her body. Once she'd recovered, Patty didn't let go of Sorcha's hand.

"I swear I'm telling ya the truth. I wanted you. You were my little angel."

Feeling more than a little scared, Sorcha tried to pull away. Her mother's face had changed and a demented expression was in her eyes.

"It was raining that night. I called to his house and the housekeeper told me to wait in the sitting room. He wasn't happy to see me but I didn't care. I threw myself at him, reminding him of the happy times we shared. I told him about you, about our angel. I asked him to give me the money to get away."

"Did he help?'

"He refused. At first. But I kept begging him. He gave it to me in the end."

"That was nice of him. But how did you get pregnant with Emer if he gave you the money to leave?"

"He was my first paying customer."

Sorcha would have fallen over if she wasn't sitting down. Horrified, she could only stare at her mother.

"Your darling pa wasn't the gentleman I thought he was. Seems he missed his little piece of Ireland. So he took what he wanted. After he was finished, he threw me out on the street. He threw some coins out with me." Patty shuddered, her eyes closed, the terror of her ordeal evident on her face. "I never told anyone what happened. I thought I could forget. But I couldn't. I had Emer to remind me. Every time I looked at that girl, I saw him. How he was that last night."

Patty threw herself into Sorcha's arms, the shuddering sobs threatening to tear her fragile body apart. Sorcha couldn't move. She held her mother until the storm of weeping passed.

"I never told anyone that before," Patty repeated. "Must be down to my time coming, I felt the need to get it off my chest."

"Didn't you tell Granny? Surely, she would have helped you?"

Patty sat in silence for a few minutes. "Sorcha, your granny was a good woman. She did the best she could for you. Father Molloy told me that. But she wasn't the type of woman who could see past her hate. I couldn't tell her I had gone to see William. She wouldn't believe he'd raped me. Nobody would. I had no choice but to leave. Having one child out of wedlock was one thing. To have another..."

The words echoed those Emer had said the day they discussed their mother. They knew their start in life had been hard but nothing would have prepared them for the truth. *Thank you, God, for making Emer so angry she didn't come to hear this.*

"So why did you come back when you heard Emer was in trouble? It must be because you love her?"

"I guess it took me a long time to realize what happened wasn't her fault. She was innocent and didn't deserve the treatment I gave her. I don't blame her for hating me. I treated her so bad."

Patty started crying again. Sorcha drew her closer, stroking her hair just like she did for Meggie when the little girl was upset.

Patty fell asleep in Sorcha's arms. Gently laying her mother down on the cot, she prayed for Patty to find a way to forgive herself. This poor creature had once been a young girl just like her. All she'd done was fall in love with the wrong man. Everything that followed was a result of that one mistake.

With a heavy heart, Sorcha left the jail house and headed toward home. Come what may, she would never tell Emer the truth of her conception. Her little sister deserved to be protected.

* * *

EMER WATCHED from a distance as Sorcha left the jailhouse. Her sister looked like the world was on her shoulders. She hated seeing her so upset.

"Sorcha, wait for me. Please."

Emer knew Sorcha had heard her as she stopped walking. Picking up her skirt, she ran down the street and grabbed Sorcha into a big hug. "I'm sorry we fought. I love you."

"I love you, too."

"Can I walk with you? Lawrence and Brian are waiting at the Sullivans'."

The sisters walked to the store in silence, both occupied with their thoughts.

"Doc told me he called to see Patty again."

"She's dying, Emer. She doesn't have long."

"Did she tell you about our fathers?"

"Father. We have the same one."

"Have? So he's alive."

"I don't know, Emer, and I don't care. You were right. We don't need anyone else. You have Lawrence, I have Brian and we have each other. "

Although she was surprised at Sorcha's reaction she was also happy. She wasn't going to visit Patty. She wanted to leave her old life in the past where it belonged. Next week, she would marry the man of her dreams and together they would face whatever challenges life would bring. With Mrs. Shipley as a mother-in-law, there were bound to be lots.

EPILOGUE

Six months later

Emer rolled the bandage around the child's arm. "That will teach you, Meggie. Climbing trees isn't a game for young ladies."|

"But Aunt Emer, you said you did everything a boy could do, only better."

"She has a point. You did say that."

Emer glared at her husband. "You aren't helping, you know."

"Sure, I am. You better be careful what you say. I don't want our daughter turning into a sharp shooter."

Emer caught his hand as he reached out to touch her belly. "How do you know the baby isn't a boy?"

He leaned in for a kiss, causing Meggie to erupt in

giggles. “Ma, come out here quick. Uncle Larry is kissing Aunt Emer. *Again.*”

Sorcha walked out of the house, her obvious pregnancy mirroring that of her sister. Lawrence moved to take the plate from her hands. "Wouldn't want you dropping any more pies."

They all laughed as Sorcha's face flushed. Emer couldn’t resist teasing her sister. "You were fairly desperate, trying to steal the attention on my wedding day."

"I didn't see Brian's foot. I swear." Sorcha tried to defend herself but they all just laughed.

"I thought you dropped the pies due to the shock of finding out my parents weren’t coming," Lawrence said putting the pie down on the picnic rug.

"Lawrence, much as I love the fact you married my sister, I do not want to spend a minute in your parents’ company. Meeting Mitchell was enough, thank you."

"Don't talk about him. I can't believe he got away without a prison sentence. It must have cost your father a fortune to make the fraud charges disappear," Emer said crossly.

"It probably did but in the long run, it would have saved Father money. He couldn’t risk having the Shipley name embroiled in charges of financial wrongdoing. I just wish he had decided to take the whole family to live in England rather than just send Mitchell. "

"Well, at least London is far away. He's not likely to turn up in Clover Springs again," Sorcha said, her face frowning with distaste.

"Sorcha, I don't believe any of my family will turn up here again."

Emer gave Lawrence a quick hug. She knew his parents' refusal to acknowledge her as his wife had hurt. She didn't care. Mrs. Shipley would miss out on knowing her grandchildren.

"Our children won't have a grandparent between them. Brian's parents died a long time ago." Sorcha took her husband's hand.

Emer looked at her sister closely. Patty's death had affected Sorcha badly. Their mother had died days before the wedding, thankfully ending the argument over whether she was attending or not. Emer let Sorcha believe she would have invited Patty to the church. As Lawrence said, it wasn't worth falling out with her sister. As it was, Emer couldn't help but think Sorcha was hiding something from her. She didn't say much about their pa but got a funny look on her face every time the subject came up. She wondered what story Patty had fed her. No doubt it was a fairytale that made Patty look innocent and the rest of the world guilty.

Her feelings toward Patty had mellowed slightly. She acknowledged the truth of Lawrence's words. If it wasn't for her mother and her past, she wouldn't have met the man she loved and have such a happy future to look forward to.

So many good things had happened in the last six months. In addition to getting married, she was carrying Lawrence's baby. Emer cradled her swelling stomach.

"Here come the Sullivans."

Emer looked up as the wagon drove in. The Sullivan men jumped down before helping their respective wives. Mary walked over to the blanket, baby Cathy asleep in her arms. Sorcha had told Emer about the baby's namesake, Mary's sister Cathy. She'd been adopted shortly before Mary came to Clover Springs. Mary still grieved for her loss.

Katie held Ella's hand. The little girl was pulling at her mother's arm.

"Let her go play with the others." Sorcha smiled at Ella. "Brian will watch out for her."

"I'll take her. Come on, brother dearest. Let's go show them how the Sullivans play ball." Daniel took his daughter's hand and walked over to where the others were playing.

Katie and Mary joined the two sisters on the blanket, Sorcha taking baby Cathy for a cuddle.

"Who'd have guessed we would all end up this happy?" Emer said to the ladies who had taken such good care of her from the first day she'd arrived in Clover Springs.

"Not Laura, anyway," Mary said, laughing.

"Who is Laura? Why wouldn't she want you to be happy?"

"Laura shared a room in the orphanage with Sorcha and I. She thought we were mad to consider becoming mail order brides. Do you remember, Sorcha? When I got that first letter from Davy. I think her exact words were he'll be ugly, smell bad and want a slave, not a wife."

"Well, she got that wrong, didn't she?" Emer said as they all looked over to their husbands. "I'm glad you didn't encourage her to come here. She doesn't sound very nice."

"Laura was sweet and kind in her own way. She didn't mean any harm in what she said. Laura was always too reserved to throw caution to the wind and come west. It was too big a risk for her to marry a man she had never met."

"Did she stay in Boston?" Emer asked.

"I guess so, although I don't know." Mary looked a little sad. "I lost contact with her after she left the orphanage. Wherever she is, I hope she is as happy as we all are."

* * *

THANK you so much for reading Emer. I hope you want to continue reading about Clover Springs. Laura, the next book brings back old friends and introduces new ones.

ACKNOWLEDGMENTS

This book wouldn't have been possible without the help of so many people. Thanks to Erin Dameron-Hill for my fantastic covers. Erin is a gifted artist who makes my characters come to life.

The ladies from Pioneer Hearts who volunteered to proofread my book. Special thanks go to Nancy Cowan, Marlene Larsen, Cindy Nipper, Marilyn Cortellini, Sherry Masters, Janet Lessley, Robin Malek, Meisje Sanders Arcuri and Denise Cervantes who all spotted errors (mine) that had slipped through.

Come join us at https://www.facebook.com/groups/rachelwessonsreaders

Last, but by no means least, huge thanks and love to my husband and my three children.

ALSO BY RACHEL WESSON

The Resistance Sisters

Darkness Falls

Light Rises

Hearts at War

When's Mummy Coming

A Mother's Promise

WWII Irish Stand Alone

Stolen from her Mother

Orphans of Hope House

Home for unloved Orphans (Orphans of Hope House 1)

Baby on the Doorstep (Orphans of Hope House 2)

Women and War

Gracie under Fire

Penny's Secret Mission

Molly's Flight

Hearts on the Rails

Orphan Train Escape

Orphan Train Trials

Orphan Train Christmas

Orphan Train Tragedy

Orphan Train Strike

Orphan Train Disaster

Trail of Hearts - Oregon Trail Series

Oregon Bound (book 1)

Oregon Dreams (book 2)

Oregon Destiny (book 3)

Oregon Discovery (book 4)

Oregon Disaster (book 5)

12 Days of Christmas - co -authored series.

The Maid - book 8

Clover Springs Mail Order Brides

Katie (Book 1)

Mary (Book 2)

Sorcha (Book 3)

Emer (Book 4)

Laura (Book 5)

Ellen (Book 6)

Thanksgiving in Clover Springs (book 7)

Christmas in Clover Springs (book8)

Erin (Book 9)

Eleanor (book 10)

Cathy (book 11)

Mrs. Grey

Clover Springs East

New York Bound (book 1)

New York Storm (book 2)

New York Hope (book 3)

Made in the USA
Las Vegas, NV
15 November 2023

80888984R00177